THE CUTTING EDGE

Also by PENELOPE GILLIATT

Novels
ONE BY ONE
A STATE OF CHANGE
Short Stories
COME BACK IF IT DOESN'T GET BETTER
NOBODY'S BUSINESS
SPLENDID LIVES
Screenplay
SUNDAY BLOODY SUNDAY
Criticism
UNHOLY FOOLS

THE CUTTING EDGE

PENELOPE GILLIATT

Coward, McCann & Geoghegan, Inc.
New York

First American Edition 1979

Copyright © 1978 by Penelope Gilliatt

Library of Congress Cataloging in Publication Data

Gilliatt, Penelope.
  The cutting edge.

  I. Title.
PZ4.G4814Cu 1979 [PR6057.I58] 823'.9'14   78-13161
ISBN 0-698-10948-1

PRINTED IN THE UNITED STATES OF AMERICA

for my sister
ANGELA CONNER

THE CUTTING EDGE

I

"It's not a nose, it's a snout," said Professor Corbett.

"I daresay it'll change," said Mrs Corbett in a nursing home, wrapping her new-born son's face away in a shawl.

"Change! No change for the better happens now."

In what he found to be a lax and dishonourable time, Professor Edward Corbett was thus awarded a boy quickly nicknamed Piggy. At the eventual christening the child was named Peregrine, but no one had the heart as he grew to call a toddler that. At kindergarten the child with the unusable name was again identified as Piggy, because the three-year-old was then a porcine shape and walked on the balls of his feet in a way that made him look as though he had trotters. It was only later, after his brother was born, that he was called Perry by the more kindly hearted of his mates at school.

The family lived in Gloucestershire. Professor Corbett, who did not believe in haste, had delayed the christening of

Peregrine and thought of him as Brother A for many months, certain that there would be another baby soon and that it would be a boy. Brother B, who was indeed a boy but was told all too soon by his beautiful mother that she had hoped for a daughter, was called Beatrice by his mother long after he could understand language. His father, then forty-nine and athletic but a man who already seemed to regard himself as a trustee of his sons rather than a parent, unexpectedly saw the wound of his wife's continuing vagueness in calling the little boy in the sailor suit by a girl's name. The Shakespearean allusion was lost on Mrs Corbett. The name Beatrice made her think of fragrant things: lilac hand soap, lavender sachets. The Professor felt more respectfully towards gender and at length announced that the then three-and-a-half-year-old was to be called Benedick.

By the time Benedick was seven, he still barely opened his mouth except to Peregrine. He was a plump little boy until then and his mother tried to make him eat less. Once when he was going to a tea party with Peregrine his mother relented and said, "You can eat as much as you want."

Benedick came back in a tempest of tears. Pressed for a reason, for once he spoke. "You said I could eat as much as I wanted and I couldn't manage it."

The silence in the nursery was so unrelenting that Mrs Corbett eventually insisted on taking Benedick to a child psychiatrist. He could find nothing wrong. Mrs Corbett never failed to emphasise to her husband the cost of the visit to London and the consultation about the child, whose only lapses from Trappist quiet were bouts of private gibberish understood only by Peregrine. He greatly resembled in looks his articulate brother. He had glossy chestnut hair quite unlike Mrs Corbett's blonde plaits or the Professor's soft white net of hair, which fluffed out like an Angora cat's when he was excited by an idea.

"Why did you take Benedick up to Harley Street?" Peregrine suddenly asked his mother when he was ten. "Has he got venereal disease?"

"What *are* you talking about?"

"I read the advertisements about clinics in tube stations. He told me the doctor was examining him for syphilis and that it runs in the family because of you. Why didn't you tell me you were a whore in the days before you married Papa?"

Mrs Corbett cut a sponge-cake grimly. "Go and get Benedick," she said. "You boys cook up too many tales."

The cherubic, dumbstruck child in the sailor suit was brought into the drawing room by their Norland nurse, who wore brown nun-like robes down to her ankles. Benedick looked not at all apprehensive.

"We'll get butter for tea this way," he said in their private language to his brother.

"What's he saying?" said Mrs Corbett to Peregrine.

"Butter for tea here. You always buy margarine for the nursery. It's all right. We know it's to prepare us for the workhouse."

"How do they know all these things about workhouses and prostitutes, Nanny?"

"They have the run of the Professor's dictionaries, Mrs Corbett. It's not my place to stop them." The nurse was a woman of termagant character who sometimes chose to pretend to haplessness. "And I can't stop them listening to the wireless, can I? There's no telling you what the BBC puts out these days. All these round-table discussions. They always

3

lead to trouble. Not to speak of the so-called Brains Trust.''

"What's a prostitute?" Benedick asked Peregrine in their private language.

"A lady with high heels and a tight satin skirt and dyed hair.''

"Oh, like the housemaids. Have you noticed the new parlourmaid's bosom?''

"What are you boys jabbering about?" said Mrs Corbett.

"Ladies. They call them intercourse on the news bulletins,'' said Peregrine.

Mrs Corbett sighed and looked at Nanny. Nanny said, "Wash your mouth out with soap and water, Master Peregrine.''

"Not with the lousy soap we get in the nursery. Mamma and Papa have French soap.''

"It's time he went to boarding school," said Nanny.

"Tomorrow we'll all go to church. You'll come?" said Mrs Corbett to Nanny.

"Forgive me, Mrs Corbett, but your church is too high for me.''

"High like the food we get in the nursery," said Peregrine.

"There's not a word of truth in the margarine story,'' said Nanny to Mrs Corbett, who didn't listen and said, "Nanny, I want you to see that the boys always get butter from now on. The Professor would be horrified.''

"The food we get in the nursery is so high it must have been in the larder for weeks," said Peregrine. "Benedick tried to use disinfectant on his shepherd's pie today. As far as the gravy we get goes, disinfectant would have been an improvement. Would you like to see his teeth? Whiter than white, because he brushes them after every meal in Pears' soap to take away the taste of the food.''

"The boys should be ready for church by ten thirty," said Mrs Corbett to Nanny, giving up.

4

"Our own mother isn't even interested in her own son's jaw," said Peregrine to the world. "I can see I'll have to pay for his false teeth later on out of the miserable salary I can make from burglaries."

At church the next morning a child chorister passed the Corbetts' pew swinging incense. Peregrine said to him, "Excuse me, but your handbag is on fire."

From an early age Peregrine put others at a disadvantage with him. His slow-burning distaste for the mediocre gave them no purchase. His loathing of the predictable led him as a prep schoolboy to several dangerous games with suicide attempts, discovering with the joy of an inventor that it was possible for him to taste life again by risking the loss of it. His chief battle was not with his tutors, or with the teasing about his name, but with the humdrum. From the age of three or so he had attacked the dulled. His one ally in the war was Benedick, who had from the beginning of his life a gift for farce. It was Peregrine's prop. But Benedick remained troubled that his brother, so stern a character, should have been born with a sense of outrage and now be nourished by it.

One New Year's Eve, when Peregrine was thirteen, he burst into the drawing room at midnight and said to an assembled house party, "The subject of the next year will be genius breaking out in the family." He took a swig of champagne. "And against the family."

Peregrine went to university and read law. At last his name was not a disadvantage to him. Benedick went to America for a while and became a rock musician. Mrs Corbett, the boys' mother, died. The only other immediate adult member of the Corbett family left to the Professor after his wife's death was the boys' aunt, Annette, who had lived with him and Mrs Corbett for years after a disastrous flit with a good-looking fishmonger whose shop was in the High Street. The fishmonger had attracted her by sympathising over the high price of salmon trout, which Professor Corbett said was the only fish that spoke to his palate. The aunt was a small, woodcock-shaped woman with pretty copper-coloured eyes and a love of yellow chiffon. She, too, died when the boys were in their early twenties. Benedick came back from America for the cremation.

"She died, aptly, of fatty degeneration of the heart," said Peregrine.

"She wasn't that bad," said Benedick. "You sometimes talk as if you were born in the eighteenth century."

"She was a good woman, in the worst sense of the term."

Benedick went into the kitchen where he had spent so much time as a child and ate the remains of a raw chocolate cake mixture from a basin. The old cook said, "All right, you're allowed, you've been away. Canada or America, was it? Everyone your age speaks with an American accent these days. It's that rock. There was a piece in the paper about a twenty-year-old girl who took herself off to a rock dance with her twelve-year-old sister. The little mite was wearing eye shadow and a perfume called 'Perhaps'."

"Surely 'Perhaps' is better than 'Certainly', as far as scent on a twelve-year-old girl goes. I mean, if I were a parent I'd be less worried."

"No, Benedick. 'Perhaps' is an invitation. An RSVP, I'd call it. Not that I'm against the young dancing. I like the Beatles. But all that rolling. The singers spit. The Beatles never spat. They'd have had good parents. But of course, it's a matter not of parents but of who you are in yourself and how.''

As life went on, Peregrine's temperament became more and more abrasive in the eyes of everyone but Benedick. He qualified as a barrister. He read enormously, with a heady excitement about originality that he chose to hide. "As Samuel Johnson said of *Gulliver's Travels*, once you've thought of the big man and the little man it's very easy to do the rest,'' he said once to Benedick, pleased by Doctor Johnson's irony. Peregrine disagreed, of course. He admired the cut of the thought but not the content of it. In his late twenties he became celebrated as a writer of journalistic broadsheets and diatribes against the modern heart. His life was like a psychological slip, disclosing the forbidden wishes that plough up an age. He was unexpectedly ready to admit himself wrong, which put people at a loss with him because they had no idea that retreat involved nothing shameful to him. It was no more than a respite, satiric in character.

"I hate peace,'' he said of himself once with respect. The remark was made to Benedick, who was not deceived. Benedick had got married early: to a tender girl with a clown's nose, named Joanna. The couple lived in Wiltshire, where Benedick made a sufficient living by playing an electronic harpsichord. It would not have been misleading, in his case, to speak of a household rather than a couple. He filled the house as a Russian might. There was conviviality, games, card tricks, meals in the middle of the night. Someone without a sense of humour there was an alien, and dislike of the foreigner would run through the house like a cold. Peregrine spent most weekends there.

"Stephen is coming to stay for Christmas," said Benedick.

"One more or less," said Peregrine, with his undeluding gloom. "Stephen was thrown into the cruel imbecility of the world at an early age."

"When we were children he used to put a whole fried egg into his mouth at breakfast when no one was looking except us."

"I liked him for that. We never gave him away. Though you were always in danger of laughing."

"How are you?"

"Lousy, thanks."

"You're not going to try to kill yourself again? It would make an unholy mess of Christmas. '

"I've decided that a man is at liberty to die only when he doesn't wish to die."

"And you don't?"

"Not on Jesus's birthday."

"I didn't know you were religious."

"Not religious, moral. You won't remember the time when science was first in the air and people talked about Darwin and monkeys." Nor could Peregrine remember it, of course, but Benedick had long understood that epochs described in books held a contemporary reality for his brother. "Our governess said that men were descended from monkeys. I told Nanny and she said it was very wicked to say such a thing."

"I didn't know you read Darwin. I remember your reading Gibbon when you were about ten."

"I didn't really read Darwin, but science was the thing then. It put me on the track."

"You'd have been on the track anyway."

"It never ceases to amaze me that people believe Church dogma. Or any dogma."

"You're very like Papa," said Benedick.

8

"In the profile, perhaps. I remember a lot of fights at home about religion when we were children. The head gardener used to roar hymns in a bellow instead of knocking at the back door when he brought in the vegetables."

"But the cook was a Baptist. She wouldn't have minded. Mamma was scared of her, you remember? Otherwise she was fearless, though vague as tulle. If one of the maids had what she called an unfortunate baby, meaning illegitimate, she always used to make a point of speaking to the young man. What's on your mind?"

"Marriage doesn't solve much." Peregrine got himself a glass of sherry and then remembered that Benedick was there too and poured him a glassful as well.

"You're not bothered so much about what you do as about what you think of what you're doing," said Benedick.

"Perhaps it's not a good theory. I haven't done very successfully in testing it yet. All I can see is other people making a muddle of things, including marriages, but without having an opinion of their actions. What about another sherry and a couple of aspirin each?"

"To ward off hangovers in advance?"

"Worth trying."

"In your view, should the aspirins be taken with water beforehand or with sherry at the time?"

"It won't make much difference once the pills are safely down the pharynx. Use sherry."

Benedick complied and was sick.

"Sorry. Water would have been better." Peregrine got him some. "At least we've found something out."

"The deductive mind," said Benedick, dead white.

"My fault. Sherry was a risk. Are you all right? I don't think I have ever cared for the smaller rashnesses. You used to thrive on them. Not that you're thriving now. Ice?"

"Why are you such a Tory when you talk? You're a born anarchist."

"Then I must be a Tory anarchist. I don't like—I don't like at all—those Hampstead liberal wets who try to solve the problem of poverty by keeping the poor alive. Or, in very extreme cases, by feeding them art. I know a rich Communist poet who arranged a lunchtime reading of his poems at a factory and turned up too late at one o'clock because he didn't know that workmen eat at twelve."

"If you're not in favour of keeping the poor alive, you want mass euthanasia?"

"I'm in favour of sense. I wouldn't kill a healthy bullock, for instance, even if it were unhappy."

"That's because you like bullocks." Benedick drank some more water. "Also people. Often."

"Do you remember the frail bullock we had that was called Cecil?"

"It was Claude. Not that either of us is in a position to find names funny."

"Mamma and Papa must have been in a bad mood every time they got near a font."

"Peregrine," said Benedick, "has the right Tory tang to it."

"Papa told me the other day that we were nearly called Eustace and Osiris. That was a narrow shave."

"Osiris would have been because of Mozart, but where did Eustace come from?"

"Probably some nineteenth-century poet favoured by Prince Albert, Papa being so hot on the nineteenth century."

An elderly first cousin once removed, named Celia, came into the drawing room with a pile of Christmas presents. "Drinking before you've even had a walk in the fresh air to put some roses into your cheeks?"

"Now that we're grown-up, the other way round seems

better," said Peregrine. "The sherry is to get up an appetite for looking at the dead rhododendrons."

Benedick said to him after Celia had gone out, "What's happened to your infant tact?"

Peregrine said, "I *never* had tact. Tact is hobbling round a subject like a donkey tied to a tree."

"It's one of the Little Lord Jesus's gifts to us, Nanny said. It's manners." The two men repeated with each other, "Manners mean not hurting other people's feelings."

Celia came back into the room and said, "And when *are* the young going out, may I ask?"

"Yes, you may. Not yet. Thank you," said Benedick.

Peregrine said to Benedick, repeating one of their nanny's jingles,

> "Children, remember that God's greatest gates
> Will open to the littlest keys;
> So remember that two of these
> Are 'Yes, I thank you' and 'If you please'."

Celia sighed, pulled her cardigan round her and plunged her right hand into one of her sagging knitted pockets. Peregrine said to Benedick, "Do you think it's colder inside or out?"

As well as the playing of electronic harpsichords, rare in Wiltshire, Benedick's garden was a topic of his heart. He showed Peregrine a newly replanted formal Elizabethan rose-garden. The parkland contained the biggest oak in England. As they had done in Gloucestershire as children, the two men clambered up several trees and then this oak, checking the circumference with linked hands. After that they went for a walk, Peregrine hating the ankle-deep soggy leaves and Benedick striding ahead. Back in the house at last, putting their Wellington boots into the cupboard under the stairs (which also held the family tennis racquets, thick socks, a Latin grammar, their father's golf clubs and his duplicate volumes of the Oxford English Dictionary), Peregrine heard the sound of crying.

"It's not Celia," he said.

"It's the twins, I suppose."

"Twins?"

"Their mother's lecturing, so we've got them." Benedick listened some more and then said, "No, it's Molly, the twins' nanny. Go and cheer her up."

"No, you go."

"You're the elder. You do realise they're Papa's illegits?"

"Brenda's twins! Why didn't you say?" Brenda had been Professor Corbett's beloved since his wife's death. Peregrine went into the nursery and found Molly weeping with her head against the mantelpiece.

"Are the kids too much for you? I must say, two at a time when their mother's in her forties and only thinks about chess is overloading it. This house is too clever by half. *Is* it the children who are troubling you?"

The nurse only sobbed more. Peregrine put his arm towards her but she pulled herself away. "This *place*," she said. "All trees. I can't get through the winter without a man." Her chin reminded Peregrine of a baby's elbow. "And then there's the spring, isn't there."

2

Sergei Sergeivitch came to the house. Seventy-seven years old but not particularly a white Russian, he liked to play ping-pong with Molly. The occasions greatly cheered her. He supported the sense of community that she loved in the house and that he found also in the spectacle of the two brothers together. The day after she had been crying out for company never known, he dropped in for a game as the sun was going down. After a time they decided to turn the match into a round-robin with Joanna, Peregrine and Benedick. Benedick played as if the game were squash and insisted that a ball counted as a winner if it came off three walls before landing on the table.

"You're playing as if this were real tennis, meaning royal tennis, with a booby trap like the Hampton Court kitchen hatch. These aren't the rules even of squash."

"I don't understand," said Molly.

"It's not a question of being able to understand Peregrine, it's a question of arguing with him or of going along with him. Depending on the energy available," said Joanna, lying down on a hammock in the cellar where they were playing. "In my case, the energy is nil. I wonder if the twins would like to go to bed?"

"No one aged two wants to go to bed," said Benedick.

"Nor do you, and you're thirty," said Peregrine. "Age tells."

"Just because you're three years older than me there's no need to talk like Methuselah. Look at Sergei." Sergei was playing a fast game alone with Molly. He stopped, sensing the right moment, and led the way up to the little living room, where Benedick's scores and electronic harpsichord took a deal of the space. Sergei smashed the bridge of his spectacles on a low Tudor beam as he came up.

"The last straw that breaks—" he said, lying down on his side and leaving the sentence unfinished like the plaster half of an ancient sculptured torso. Joanna took the spectacles from him and mended them with a strip of sticking tape.

"Can you see?" she said. "Can you see this bottle of vodka?"

"If I shut one eye. Then if I shut the other eye I can see the jar of pickled cucumbers I brought over. No one else seems to have noticed them. Oh, the grief of it all. Never mind. Might we have a pickled cucumber or two with our vodkas? Might we have the twins down by the fire?"

Sergei had long ago been an exiled theatrical impresario in America. He had an inborn gift for the congenial. The twins lay quiescent in identical positions by the fire. Their names were Sam and Tom. Tom ate greedily from his bottle of milk but Sam pushed the rubber teat away.

"He's losing weight," said Molly. "He won't drink."

Sergei said, "Try feeding him from a jug. I think he feels as if he's suffocating when he's forced towards that bottle." The jug method worked. Sergei began to talk to Molly while Benedick was improvising on the harpsichord and Peregrine was reading the score of something quite different.

"They are such a wonderful two people," said Sergei about

the brothers to Molly. "They should both be in the theatre, because it happens that theatre is an allegoric idea of what life can be like. It is often theatre that makes the *putsch*."

"It was the revolution that made you go to America?"

"No. I am a pink Russian. I left only in 1925. I came with a group of students who were involved in a company called The Study of Life. If you could hear the words in Russian!" He repeated them, in a voice like Chaliapin's. The brothers stopped what they were doing to listen to him. He wore pointed shoes, black and white spongebag trousers, a maroon jacket and a yellow shirt. "We did shows in Geneva. Chekhov, Gorki. Fourteen or fifteen performances. Then we went to America and I developed a crazy big dream of music hall and plays and operas all mixed up in a huge theatre. The organ was to play quite a large part. Well, the trouble was we had no theatre. So we went on the road and saved and someone told me about a space for rent in Manhattan. A space is what theatre people call experimental theatre, you understand. Another pickled cucumber? We were not at all experimental, I have to tell you. We simply liked to perform in this interesting new country, which it has just occurred to me is the only country that was longed for before it was really populated. A question of envisagement. We decided to do *Madame Butterfly*. There was difficulty over the business and because we had to cut it. So I called Puccini's son in Rome and he said, 'Oh, that's all right.' The question is to go to the top. The busiest people are always the ones who give you the quickest answers. Our *Butterfly* ran an hour. Fifty minutes, maybe. It sank down very well. We had eleven *legitimate* curtain calls. We ran it for three weeks, four times a day. The stage was a hundred and four feet wide so we had to condense it with flats drawn in from the wings for a wonderful double act with a dog that came before *Butterfly*. The dog sat still because that was his act so the performers were on the sprint to keep things moving. Of course, the truth is that their talent could have filled the stage but I was too young to know that. They became quite famous. None of you would have heard of them because now *you're* too young and they're dead."

"The dead are indestructible," said Peregrine.

He *is* religious, thought Benedick and Joanna.

"No, I'm not," said Peregrine, picking up their thoughts. "Once again you're confusing religious and moral. I gave up on religion when I was told at Sunday School that there are some things, such as the Trinity, that have to be accepted as unfathomable mysteries."

"After that," said Sergei, "I stumbled on the idea of regimental dancing by pretty young women in tights. All in rhythm, you understand. I discovered a group called the Tippy-Toes. What a fund of relief they were! The people who didn't want *Butterfly* came for the Tippy-Toes and vice versa. We also had five shepherds whom we regularly used after a short version of *Carmen*. A little magnitude is a fine refreshment on stage. I knew Roxy, the great impresario. I daresay you've heard of him. Everything he did had mass. A toast to the indestructible! I'm looking at Sam. Keep to the jug method is my advice. Some people have an aversion to what ordinary minds call the life instinct. Sucking a bottle is said to be basic but it's the exceptions who interest, don't you find?"

Joanna came into the room with some hot sausages. "Aha! England's answer to the pickled cucumber," said Sergei. "Am I talking too much, old friends? I must just tell you about some of the difficulties. It's all been trumpet-blowing. One of the great nuisances was the question of the religious shows. Easter, Christmas. In the case of religion, the theatre is full of pitfalls. It's like the army. If you put on one stripe too few you get people saying everything's wrong. In New York I planned the show and then went to every denomination in the city until they all approved. Yom Kippur was a problem. I couldn't have the solo cantor. It means so much to Jews. You might say I was an apprentice in everything.''

"Aren't we all," said Benedick.

"I'd always thought you were a dentist originally," said Molly to Sergei.

"I studied in Geneva but I never qualified. I was never allowed to do operations. Too busy studying showmanship. Ah, the worthlessness of it all! But it repays recall, in the company of friends. A toast!" He drank some more vodka. "Father was an agent of wheat. He wouldn't have approved of the Tippy-Toes. He had very nice hair, I remember. He was quite a ladies' man. He'd have liked my theatre. It was all gold. The backer's wife was very interested in gold. She once gave me a stuffed fish entirely encrusted in gold. Why a fish, I don't know. I think she liked a show I thought up about Russian life. It was in three parts. The religious part was in front of a church.''

"And you played a simpleton, I remember your saying," said Molly.

"I could always do village idiots. Now here I am, in the last decade of my life, I assume, doing the same thing in Wiltshire, of all places. What's Benedick playing?''

"He's improvising music for your Russian tableau," said Peregrine.

"The second scene was a Russian wedding. Pretty, you know. The last scene was a gypsy scene. So there you had these three varieties of colour, people, mood. There was the difficulty that we were speaking Russian but Americans are very kind to people who don't speak English. Once we had to go to a convent. A man's convent. Yes, a monastery. Well, at this monastery I had to get eight acts out of forty-six people.

They had beautiful costumes. The monks prepared a wonderful Russian dinner. I spoke English like a Spanish cow. I played my usual simpleton.'' He did a fool's dance for them for a moment or two before collapsing back into his armchair. His movements were a young man's. "Excuse me.'' He caught his breath, and then said, "I also played a, how do you call it here, receptionist. Because he does a lot of writing and I had the small ability to make writing notes theatrical on quite a big stage. But I have to tell you that once I sang Tchaikovsky to a full symphony orchestra. It was the greatest thrill of my life. I beg your pardon.'' He passed the vodka bottle. "We had great dormitories where the Tippy-Toes could sleep between shows. It was almost like a little world. No, a big world. We knew we were doing the right thing because the audience was happy. Money was short when we were on the road but the feeling we had wasn't fearful, it was one of accomplishment. We didn't want a comfortable existence. Nothing came our way then like this harpsichord and the twins and so on. Etcetera, etcetera. I'm not earning my keep in the world at the moment, that's a fact, but there's not anything I have to supply that people want now. It's time I stepped aside, in any case. Oh, my friends, I *am* having a nice time! I wonder what vocation the twins will find. Good listeners, eh? Not a squeak out of them all the time I've been rambling. Now I shall leave you and do my income tax. It's not difficult when there's just yourself to account for.''

3

Five years later, with the twins staying at Benedick's, Professor Corbett was once talking to Sergei. They were speaking of figures in *Ulysses*.

"Isn't it plausible that they hadn't had intercourse all those years?" said Professor Corbett.

Sergei said, "It isn't clear that they hadn't had intercourse." Then, delicately, "Only perhaps that they hadn't, so to speak, finished."

"Oh," said Professor Corbett. "You don't say."

"Who knows?"

They were speaking of Joyce as if the characters were in the house. The house was very small, and the tall Corbetts constantly struck their heads against the Tudor beams. The telephone had been cut off because Benedick hadn't been able to pay the bill.

"Do you happen to have seen my socks?" asked Professor Corbett. "They had garters on them because they were only worn for three hours yesterday and they seemed good for another day. After being out of pyjamas and into them so soon, washing the socks seemed a waste of laundry. Then, to go on about Joyce, there's the question of the Hungarian

Jewishness. The man isn't like any Hungarian Jew I've met."

"You speak Hungarian?"

"The glottal stop presents problems but it's a joy to master."

"I'll ask Joanna about your socks." Joanna came into the room. Professor Corbett said, "Thank goodness waists have come back. In the old days when I could do a César Franck tenth on the piano, I could have put my hands around your waist. Now I'm looking for my socks."

Joanna said in Russian that she hadn't seen them.

"That's one of the things I like about her. She keeps up Russian for me," said Sergei. "French, Russian, Spanish, Italian, Portuguese, Norwegian, English. Is there any language you don't speak?"

"I'd like to be able to speak Polish and Czech. I once had an affair with a man in the Foreign Service who was a Slav expert and he muddled me by telling me the words in Polish and Czech before he told me the Russian."

"I don't hear you," said Professor Corbett. Joanna repeated herself, facing him so that he could see her lip movements.

"I daresay Serbo-Croat was a cinch," said Sergei. "Did you find the Cyrillic alphabet a trial? I once considered calling a child Cyril but my late English wife didn't see the churchly connections. She said that any child called Cyril was going to turn out to be an accountant or a toll-keeper."

He sat down on the side of his usual armchair and said, "What's for lunch? How are you off for money? I daresay I could coax myself into having a little flutter on the two of you. And the other thing is, a pair of Wellingtons would do perfectly in place of the socks, wouldn't they? Then we'd all be ready for a walk, if called for."

Joanna said, "In the first case, steak and kidney pudding. In the second case, we're fine." She moved towards him and banged her head against a beam. She was five foot ten and wore bangles above her elbows over her thick Welsh sweater. "In the third case," turning to the Professor, "there are plenty of Wellingtons but you must promise to borrow some of Benedick's socks before you go out."

"My friend Brenda always wanted a daughter and I would say a tall daughter but I don't seem to be up to anything but sons," said Professor Corbett. "Do you think the twins will be as fond of each other as Peregrine and Benedick? Look at them. They're already different, of course. Tom beginning to speak, Sam not."

Tom raised himself on one elbow, looking oddly elderly, and said, "Sam talks to me. He talked to me lasterday."

Joanna said in French to the Professor, "I can't think how their mother can have left them when they say such fine things as that."

The Professor spread his hands and said, "I miss her, you know. But wounds are delivered so that we remember we were here."

The steak and kidney pudding was eaten. In the middle of it a bell rang. It wasn't, of course, the cut-off telephone, nor the doorbell. The Professor made a move: slowly, because of his arthritis. Joanna jumped up.

"It'll be for me." She ducked her head to avoid the beams and ran to a little room that the Professor had never explored.

"Don't follow her, she doesn't like it," said Benedick.

"*Politesse* has less force than wanting to find things out, to my eye," said the Professor.

He found Joanna operating a Telex machine in Spanish. A Telex machine, in this old Tudor house? The room was no bigger than a bathroom, scattered with Telex messages in many languages. She was conducting a deal for fifteen hundred jeeps to be sent from Uruguay to the Middle East. The machine clattered. The negotiation was quickly closed.

"Is this what you both live on?" said the Professor.

"Benedick doesn't like my doing it."

"But you do."

"It's money for the twins. I've opened a bank account."

"Are you in the CIA?"

"No. I swear. I just enjoy the work, that's all. I'd go mad in the country if I weren't doing this. It's a way of travelling. At any minute I can be in the Middle East or India or Latin America."

"Does Peregrine know?"

"I don't think so. He doesn't like women working."

"You've got a very old-fashioned idea of the sort of man he is."

"He prefers women like that blasted Catherine von what's-her-name."

"The woman who looks as if she couldn't lift a finger." The Professor turned to go and said as he left, "Or know how to have it lifted for her. This Telex is to keep your mind off worrying about leaving Benedick, isn't it? He'll be all right. Corbetts are. It's you I'm bothered about. You rely too much on stamina. I once knew a race horse that had already beaten all the records and his owner kept him racing until he was thirteen. He couldn't bear to be beaten, that horse. The mortification. Blood was coming from every orifice."

"My life, whose else, first version," said Joanna.

"Of course, you *hold* with the world."

That evening Benedick told Peregrine over a game of dominoes that Joanna had decided to leave him.

"Why?"

"She feels out of touch with the world. She's giving me custody of Brenda's children with Papa because Brenda can't cope. Joanna's making a mistake in going, I believe. She's wrong, but I did wrong not to know she was light-headed."

"In no way."

"Compare her with Molly," said Benedick.

"Values can't be measured against each other. They're incommensurable. They allow no reduction below themselves. One may prefer Dante to Shakespeare, or claret to champagne, but that ends it."

Benedick was silent.

"Choices are underived."

Benedick's silence still hung in the air like a dead pheasant.

"My poor boy."

"I'm not a boy."

"But I'm the elder, and the odd thing is that I seem to be more carefree than you are."

"It's better when you stop talking like a translator from Rumanian. I lose you then, and it's worse than losing Joanna. I can't bear being dependent on her."

That night, when Joanna was sleeping on the sofa, Benedick crept down to her and offered her an extra eiderdown.

"Aren't you sleeping? You're shivering like a dog."

"I thought you might be cold."

He said again, as he had said to his brother, "I can't bear being dependent on you." Angrily, "I want you out of the house by tomorrow lunchtime."

"Lunchtime! Who'll get lunch? I can't pack up a life of seven years in three hours."

23

"There are always sardines. You wouldn't change your mind? Give up the Telex?"

"I can't. It's absurd to be jealous of a Telex."

"I can't share you with a machine. Locked away."

"It's only like your harpsichord. I'm sorry. I feel pent up. I don't want the shrapnel to hit people."

"Are you having an affair?"

"No."

"The Telex only means I'm not giving you enough."

"Often you have."

"No point in disguising the lack. Solving the problem by sweeping the dominoes off the table." Benedick went up to their room and tried listening to records, but someone had been meddling with the machine and the needle kept going back to the arm-rest.

At breakfast early next morning he talked – not very much – to Peregrine. "I daresay it's for the best. The harpsichord was getting on her nerves. Joanna moves too fast for me. Or perhaps I should have said that I move too slowly for her."

"People hold the race is not always to the swift. Why?"

"Well, it's a comforting cliché. It usually gets a hand."

"But why isn't it? Why isn't the race to the swift?"

"It is, but the slow like being told that sloth doesn't matter. The accepted rubric of opinion."

Tom tottered purposefully into the room and said, "Joanna's gone to church."

"Women as the accomplice of religion and superstition," said Peregrine to Benedick, and then, to Tom, "Was she wearing a hat? I could almost pray, 'No, please God', you know how I hate hats."

"A black handkerchief. I expect it was to keep her ears warm. I said she could have my ear muffs but she didn't want them."

"Lot of Utopian gas," said Benedick to Peregrine. They played tobogganing on a tea tray with the boys on the stairs, carefully guided by Benedick behind them and by Peregrine holding Sam upright because even in the middle of play he was inclined to lie down to take a doze.

"Damn Joanna," said Peregrine.

"A poor and galling consolation to damn her when you're not at church."

"Doesn't 'damn' hold good outside the sacred portals?"

"I daresay. I feel like a go on the tray myself now." Peregrine manoeuvered the stairs as if he were in a slalom race, and then gave up the tray to Benedick, who took off his shoes for the sake of the tray and then caught his right toes in one of the stair-railings. He took off his sock and looked at the toe, which was bent sideways.

"A right-angled toe. I can't get it back into position."

"It's broken. The only thing to do is to strap it to the one next to it," said Peregrine. "I'll get some sticky tape."

"Will I be able to use the harpsichord?" Benedick started to laugh. "A broken marriage and a broken little toe, in whatever order occurs to the good Lord. It hurts."

"I don't believe for a moment she's at church. More likely at a palmist," said Peregrine. He had not only a roll of sticking plaster with him but also a couple of matches. "The matches are to get the toe adjusted to being straight. Like a splint."

"I wish Joanna would be direct with me."

"She's doing what she can, I think." In Latin, "She knows she'd be no good helping Papa out with the children."

"I've forgotten Latin. Say it in musical terms."

"Never mind. Children, Benedick has broken his little toe. Go and tell your father about the accident."

"Would he know a toe-mender?" said Tom.

"It's just to keep him in touch. Ask him what he'd like for breakfast. Sam, why didn't you eat anything?"

"The sun was in my eyes."

"It's nice and dark on the stairs. I'll get Sam his favourite."

Tom came back with a Crown Derby plate carrying some cold mashed potatoes and a chocolate biscuit. Then he disappeared again and stumbled up the stairs with two more Crown Derby plates, two more lots of cold mashed potatoes and two more chocolate biscuits for Benedick and Peregrine. "I'm sorry I was long. Two plates is broken. The fridge handle got in the way. That's two broken plates, one broken toe and one broken marriage. What is a broken marriage exactly?"

"When something goes wrong between a husband and wife. It doesn't mean anybody's done anything bad, it just means they're not making each other happy."

"But the fishmonger is all right."

"Absolutely."

When the children had disappeared into the old man's room, Peregrine said to Benedick, "You mustn't blame Joanna."

"I do. I think she's behaving carelessly to the point of crime. And what's more somebody's messed up my Hi-Fi and I don't see who it could be but her because it's beyond the reach of the twins."

"Perhaps she was playing something to cheer herself up. She's casual but nothing worse. Some people act all right but their actions can have a bad echo. Or they may blunder like Joanna but still have a good echo."

4

Joanna's divorce came through. Benedick and Peregrine went to Istanbul: to the Asian side, where wooden and magnificent unpainted houses lay along the shore. They found, for very little money, a house that became their best loved home. It had pillars on a terrace overlooking the Bosphorus and a pleasantly confused garden of long grasses and a mixture of wild and cultivated flowers. A beautiful stone sundial had toppled into the unmown lawn and lay on its side, half-hidden but significant, like a page turned down in a valuable old volume. Portraits of family ancestors hung on the walls. Whose family? The brothers themselves never met the owner. They grew to know the sloping shoulders of the Victorian women in the portraits, the medals on the chests of the ferociously good-looking men, as though they constituted the insignia of a family they had always been looking for. Of their own parents they felt themselves to be the bastard heirs. This was where their true ancestry lay, in the huge rooms with dust sheets over the sofas in the drawing room, dust sheets that they never took off. The light was sometimes powdery, sometimes brilliant. The house was full of reflections from the Bosphorus outside. Benedick one day took the dust sheet off what was clearly a harpsichord and tuned the instrument himself, patiently bringing it up to pitch half a tone a day.

The brothers earned a living by teaching at a language school. Neither of them spoke a word of Turkish, but the school's method was for the tutors to speak only in the tongue they were teaching. Benedick was always on time and taught a vivacious sort of English. Peregrine was perpetually late in coming and in going, and taught a more startling and suddenly stately English. The school was run by an Englishwoman named Mrs Sparks, a title ill.suited to her lack of spontaneity. One day she spoke to Peregrine about his unpunctuality. He replied by sliding down the bannisters. Next day he hired a boat and taught his class on the Bosphorus. Mrs Sparks was baffled by his inventiveness and told him off.

"Mrs Sparks," said Peregrine to Benedick, "has been what they called at school 'speaking to me'."

"She's all right."

"Yeasty good will."

Benedick kept his brother in good humour and also in funds. Peregrine went back to writing rhetoric to his fellow-countrymen, and began his own vein in polemic poetry. He was one of the elect who locate and initiate the conscience of their countrymen. The broadsheets made him celebrated: the poetry came back with rejection slip after rejection slip.

"We could paper this room with them," said Peregrine.

"We're not going to change a thing," said Benedick.

"You've altered the harpsichord. That's work," said Peregrine, looking at the Bosphorus.

"So are rejection slips. Or rather, non-work, which is the same thing. Polarity is often concord. Yes and no are very finely divided."

"It's only the Western philosophers who can concoct argument out of disagreement."

"All I know is that your poems are fine."

"Could you stand hearing a new lot? They're not up to much. I can't think of a title for them. One is going to get me into trouble because it questions the money spent on the Royal Family and another is going to get me into trouble because it questions the dopey English passion for having dogs sleep on the bed."

Benedick listened, laughing now and then at intentional anti-climaxes, and then said, "They'd be published in a minute. I've written a song-cycle. Would you write the words?"

Next evening he and Peregrine walked up and down outside the post office arguing about whether to send the poems to an English publisher. Peregrine dropped the manuscript into the gutter by mistake and looked down at it as though the fall were an omen. The string had come apart, the brown paper had broken.

"That settles it."

"I'll mend it with sticking plaster. I must say sticking plaster seems to enter life a good deal."

"Where would we get sticking plaster on the Bosphorus?"

"I've got it in my pocket, in case of emergencies."

"Don't be a nanny to me."

"You live in a permanent state of emergency."

"All right, it's curfew. I'm throwing in my hand."

Benedick had mended the parcel as they were talking. "Come on, let's send it off."

"It's not to the heart of things."

"But it'll get published, and then the next books will be easier."

"What's that letter sticking out of your pocket?"

29

"Throwing in my hand to my agent about English engagements. I've decided to be your secretary. If I may. So that we can be together and I can compose on the spot."

"What?"

"I've got a harpsichord here, after all. And we do get on."

"There's another of those bloody cats. Why is Istanbul full of cats? I can hear them making judgements. Dogs don't judge. Cats are perpetual moral arbiters." Peregrine kicked one, which ran off to a corner in the street and came to a sudden stop to look back at them.

The brothers posted the book manuscript and the letter, bartering the rights of doing both or neither like small boys. The book was accepted and it sold out. In a way Peregrine had been right, because the book was not on the rails of the future work he had in mind. In a way Benedick had been right, because publication of this book made the next one easier.

As the brothers went about their business, the cats stared at them from everywhere.

"I can't have you wasting your life on being my secretary," said Peregrine, sitting on the terrace with his brother.

"I'm afraid I'm a man with only one idea."

"What is it?"

Benedick was as silent as he had been as a child. Peregrine repeated the question in their childhood gibberish, with no luck, and then went to have a solitary drink in his work room above. A steamer passed on the Bosphorus. A thin little girl of about fourteen, who worked in the house, came into the room to ask what laundry she could do. Peregrine made love to her, each speaking to the other in an unknown tongue. A chandelier, unlit, hanging from the dusty domed ceiling caught reflections of light from the Bosphorus.

"Thank you," said Peregrine in English, knowing she wouldn't understand. "I'm sorry I wasn't much good. I was nervous."

The girl lay happily in his arms, touching him, believing that all was well. She laughed, hiding her head in his chest.

"I wonder what the legal age for seducing a minor is in Turkey?" said Peregrine in English, stroking her hair.

"I wonder if you've ever made love to a girl before in a language you don't understand," said the maid in Turkish. Peregrine touched her thin shoulder blades, which were almost as soft and small as bird's wings, and knew she was asking him something crucial. She could find no way to put it into a message he would understand and only got up to point to the shelves of his chest of drawers to ask him about the laundry. He got up and bathed her fondly in his beautiful tile-lined Turkish bath, not troubling to dress. There were looking-glasses everywhere, reflecting the ever-present Bosphorus, and he marvelled at her tiny nubile body.

"This is what London must have looked like before the Great Fire in 1666," he said in English about the wooden houses on the shore as they stood in front of the window in bath towels. "All unpainted wooden houses turned ash-grey with the weather, and people using the Thames as a main road." Rubbing the frail girl dry, he looked down at the garden and saw a cat gazing at them.

5

Professor Corbett, Molly and the twins arrived next year to stay with the brothers. The old man said to Benedick that he found Peregrine changed.

"He's changed his profession. He's also drinking too much. Not a great deal too much. He stops when he's working. It's interesting, isn't it, the instinct that people have to protect what's most valuable to them? I really think he may be a great writer."

"What about his profession?"

"Writing is his profession."

"He's turning people against him."

Peregrine came into the room and said, "Alienation is a cant tag for a necessary position."

The Professor said, "You always had an inciting personality."

Peregrine sat down in an eighteenth-century tapestry chair with a dust sheet over it and pulled the cloth around him. His father said, "You're doing things at the cost of others. Also, what you're inciting is only a sense of sterility and stalemate. There's none of your old-turbulence. Only a ravenous feeling that you've been emptied. That you're full of dead air. You're living on old spites, lacking even energy.

You'll be all right, of course. A spirit like yours is beyond ruin. But I couldn't help observing that your last book was dedicated 'To my friends'. You haven't got any friends, apart from Benedick. You haven't got any life. You're very lonely, aren't you? You drive away your friends to prove how treacherous man is." The old man walked across the room to look at the Bosphorus, hiding the fact that he was weeping. "It's true that you have no friends, isn't it?" he said again, blowing his nose on a beautiful old French cotton handkerchief.

"He has a great friend here in the house," said Benedick defensively.

"I haven't been introduced, unless you mean yourself."

"She works here."

"One must take great care in mixing the classes. People who think themselves to be without class consciousness are generally the fortunate. Only the underprivileged notice that condescension, and they are apt to strike back."

Benedick said, "It's in some people's nature to be piratical."

What was to his father the evidence of mutiny in Peregrine was to Benedick the result of old sadnesses. Eliding over this thought, which both brothers knew their father would have caught, Peregrine said, "You're speaking as if I were a profane and surfeited old man. You don't understand. I want to live in a margin of private life."

The Professor waited, and then said, "You really think I don't know that?"

"I had a deceiving infancy."

"And who also did?"

"Benedick."

"And who rescued him from it?"

No one answered.

"You, Peregrine, of course. You're in a dream that you've

33

got to shake off. A dream of being cheated. I can see the future as clearly as the past but insights are no use to you.''

''I don't need much insight to see that you and Molly have made it together.''

''She's a very remarkable girl. I wish we had met each other at more nearly the same age. I can't ask anything of a young girl. All I can do is pretend to be an old dodderer. Of course, the truth is we all feel ourselves to be all ages at all times. I suppose the twins aren't frightened in this rickety house? I once knew a foal who was kept beside a lake and who taught himself to swim like a dog, but the twins aren't like that.''

The twins were now upstairs doing homework under Molly's tutorship. She had been teaching Tom biology and botany. Peregrine called up to the little boys, who were sitting on next-door steps with their legs through the spaces between the stair-rails, and said, ''What are you doing?''

Tom said, ''I know what I'm doing but I don't know what it's called.''

The Professor said to Peregrine when he came back, after a pause, ''You realise the losses in private that public power entails. You've become a very powerful element in public life.''

Public life struck back by disbarring Peregrine because of the evidence inquirers had collected about his illegal love for the little laundry-maid. By now the Establishment was angry with him for surviving and indeed prospering outside the accepted rules. The Bar Association decided to keep the business away from the press, knowing to the hilt the Establishment law that a spy who is found out is to be disowned.

''It doesn't matter, anyway,'' said Peregrine to his father

34

upon getting official notice that he was barred from legal practice. He seemed, in fact, almost invigorated. "I'm a poet. I'm going to be a great poet, if fortune turns my way. At the moment I apologise for my state. It's like filling the house with lost causes and lame dogs."

"Not at all," said his father. "But be careful of Benedick."

The family played games at night with each other. One evening Benedick invented a game with his brother in mind. It lay in giving the players a situation to recount and seeing which one had the most votes for being publishable. The situation was that a wife was to be told by her New York psychiatrist that her husband had had a particular accident. The dialogue had to be psychiatric in character. Peregrine's version won. It went like this:

The psychiatrist: You know how an air conditioner works?
The woman: Roughly.
The psychiatrist: It has to stick out of the window and be very carefully fitted so that the air flow is constant into the cooling system, which is heavy.
The woman: Polluted air?
The psychiatrist: Your husband has been hospitalised. You're reacting with laughter. What does that tell us?
The woman: My husband's in hospital because of pollution?
The psychiatrist: The air conditioner works by a very interesting system. I could draw you a diagram but our fifty minutes is nearly up. The happy thing about air conditioners, visually speaking, is that they look like Corbusier additions to the building. They have the same visual appeal as, say, the fire escapes in Harlem that were caught so wonderfully by Oliver Smith in *West Side Story*.

The woman: The fire escapes are to escape from fire. What about my husband?

The psychiatrist: It's important to have your air conditioner serviced every year because of the accumulated smog and dirt that collects in the coils of the system. The best time to get your air conditioner serviced is in January when everyone has heating, not cooling, on his mind. Or hers.

The woman: My husband?

The psychiatrist: As I say, he's been hospitalised. It's quite serious.

The woman: Serious?

The psychiatrist: Very serious.

The woman: He's dead?

The psychiatrist: Air conditioners are household items, as I said. They should always be installed by professionals. Your husband took a walk along Fifth Avenue today.

The woman: A mugging?

The psychiatrist: Your husband was hit on the head.

The woman: Did they catch the man?

The psychiatrist: Your husband was hit quite severely on the head by a falling air conditioner.

The woman: "*Quite* severely?"

The psychiatrist: Very severely. He's dead.

The Professor's version, though most earnestly intended to eschew the humour of the misplaced climax, started at the wrong end typical of the non-fiction writer and went like this:

The psychiatrist: I'm afraid I have very bad news for you this session. Your husband was hit on the head by an air conditioner and he's dead. Now we'll investigate our reactions.

The woman: Where is he? I must go.

The psychiatrist: We must learn to accept reality. Your husband is dead.

The woman: How can an air conditioner kill a man? What shall I do next?

The psychiatrist: You see, already the human mind is protecting itself. We're thinking of our next husband.

Molly's version was swift and attacked the problem of the death's perilously humorous content.

The psychiatrist: Your husband has been fatally injured by a falling air conditioner.

The woman: Which hospital?

6

When Papa, Molly and the twins left the Bosphorus, Peregrine found himself bereft. His sense of exile was compounded by an unidentified but English-speaking voice on the telephone.

"You won't remember my name," said the voice.

"What is it?"

"Robin Redding. I changed it from Sidney Hustle."

"I'm sorry?"

"Robin Redding. What's the matter?"

"It's all right, I'm here. I'm sorry I don't remember you."

"Hustle is what I'm not."

"What?"

"I mean I'm not a hustler."

"You sound well-named."

"Think of me as Robin."

"Perhaps I didn't get your surname right."

"I wondered what you were doing this weekend."

"I'm going away, I'm afraid."

"Never mind."

"What?"

"That can be managed."

"Eh?"

"I know you're interested in the French cinema."

"I wonder if you're thinking of someone else?"

"I remember you very well. I've invited everyone around Cannes."

"Who?"

"I've asked Elliott Stein."

"Oh. Who's Elliott Stein?"

"He's not coming."

Peregrine put down the telephone receiver with the feeling that he didn't exist. He told Benedick the story, with perfect recall. Benedick responded at first in a practical way.

"Was he a burglar? I'll tell the police."

"Only a very inventive burglar would say that he'd met me at a stinking film festival."

"What have you got against film festivals?"

"Canapés and opportunists."

"What?"

"What I say. Film festivals are cattle fairs with perks for go-getters. I once knew a penniless and talentless young man who somehow wormed himself into getting into every film festival in Europe with a free hotel room and an exhausting diet of canapés at foreign delegation parties. Film festivals are all over the place. This chap got himself to some place in Belgium over Christmas Day itself. He said Yugoslavia was a cinch for cartoon maniacs and that Czechoslavakia couldn't be beaten for invitations to puppet festivals. In fact, now I come to think of it, he printed my name as a judge of a puppet film festival without asking me. I've got to tell you something. I thought of going to Positano. I've got to get away."

"You mean away from me."

"Never that." After a pause, "Trusty and well-beloved."

"As they say on military awards."

"It always struck me as being like something in the prayer book. The other place I could go is America."

"I thought you didn't like tall buildings."

"I shouldn't go because of the buildings. It's the American turn of mind that interests me. Interests me rather than consoles me. I'm not in need of consoling."

"I should stay in Europe."

"I'm getting too dependent on you," said Peregrine, sneezing a good many of what the brothers calculated to be his usual average of thirteen times. He had never tracked down the cause. Not women's scent, not the brackish wine that he was sipping while Benedick put away half a bottle of slivovic which he had bought in Yugoslavia on one of his many healing voyages since the loss of Joanna.

Benedick kept the house on the Bosphorus, to which Peregrine presented him with the deeds almost as if they were a dowry. He taught his illegitimate half-brothers about the history of the Balkans, which they absorbed with as much interest as if they were learning hopscotch. The aging Professor Corbett came out again to be with Molly. He was getting used to being without his unmarried Brenda, who was now fast in love with dead Aunt Annette's irresistible fishmonger. Brenda and he had had some absurd fight over a silver tea service and candlesticks on the long distance telephone.

"They're the Corbett family's. You're not a Corbett," Professor Corbett had said.

"No woman is truly anything with this business of changing your name when you get married. The point is, I shaved the ends of the candles so that they'd fit into the bleeding Georgian holders. Those candlesticks were made for Ethelred the Unready to put burning tapers into, if you ask me."

"What an interesting idea."

Idea was a word for special occasions by any of the Corbetts.

Benedick, with Peregrine gone to Positano, taught his half-brothers to swim. They took to water as if it were an element more natural to them than air. Then Benedick said to them that it was an interesting idea to dive. He showed them. Sam tumbled in without trouble. Tom tried and failed the first time.

"What's the big mydea?" he said.

Tom was as tacitly precise as Benedick had been as a small boy. He was asked by a visitor if he were four years old.

"No."

"Five?"

"Not exactly."

"Why not exactly?"

"I shall be five in two days' time."

Benedick was soon to lose the children, who were to go back to England with Molly and the Professor.

"I've seen the Asian side, I've seen the European side. I've seen everything I want to see, speaking architecturally and religiously," said the Professor. "I can feel old Constantinople, ancient Byzantium itself, as they used to be, but hidden. I find it rather upsetting, like seeing only the upper excavations of Troy and knowing nothing about the six cities below. But Molly enjoyed everything and so did the twins. She had never been abroad before she first came to Turkey, apart from a day trip to Dieppe before the war. It was a marvellous thing to see, her Memling eyes and her excitement."

"I thought you said she'd been to Venice," said Benedick.

"Ah, that was on our way here. She really likes steak and chips and tea but she bravely followed the children's example with snails in garlic butter and so forth. One night when she'd been particularly good about *fettuccine alla linguine* I ordered her a *cappuccino.*''

Molly had come into the room. ''Cup of what, darling?''

A steamer hooted on the Bosphorus outside and to Benedick it sounded like a doorbell signalling the end of a celebration. ''Festivities can't go on all night,'' he said, as much to himself as to the Professor or Molly. Both of them understood him. ''Will you see Peregrine in Italy?'' he said. ''Will you ask him to write?''

''You miss him, don't you,'' said Molly.

''He's my brother.'' That explained enough.

''You're very like Sam and Tom.''

''We agreed when we were children that he'd do the talking to other people. And the thinking, of course. We left music and mechanical things to me because someone gave us a toy xylophone for Christmas and Peregrine bust one of the keys and I mended it.''

''You've been mending his ramshackle life as long as I can remember,'' said the Professor. ''You're the only one who has ever managed it.''

''A life like Peregrine's can't easily be put back in pitch.''

That night, alone in the house, Benedick wandered about, played the harpsichord, and made a list of the elements in his life, divided under the headings of ''Soluble'' and ''Insoluble''. Under ''Insoluble'' he put ''Marriage'', ''Quarter-tones'', ''Dinner parties'' and ''Barber''. Under ''Soluble'' he put ''Peregrine'', ''Piano-tuning'', ''Pieces for harpsichord'', ''Growing things'' and ''Making a Living''.

7

Professor Corbett, back in Gloucestershire, was writing a book about Turkey, which he knew better from scholarship than from his time with Benedick. He and Molly lived in sin, said neighbours: all of his old acquaintances but one, a retired Army man who existed with his wife on a small pension. She was in the habit of leaving two hot-water bottles in the Professor's and Molly's bed if they had ever been away for the weekend with the now school-aged twins and were due to return to the cold great house. At one such time the children raced ahead of them and made an apple-pie bed for them. The Professor was irked. Molly laughed.

"What made you do something so tedious?" he asked the boys in his library. Sam looked at Tom and spoke in gibberish just as Peregrine and Benedick had before them.

"Speak *English*!" roared their father, banging his fist on the desk.

"We thought it would make you laugh," said Tom.

"Fitful. Wilful. Childish."

Molly said to the Professor, "Well, they are children. I daresay it was ambiguous."

"What's ambiguous?" Sam asked of Tom.

"I expect it's one of those things that make people wonder," said Tom.

"They'd better go to boarding school," said the Professor.

"They need home," said Molly.

"They need boarding school. We could choose a progressive one."

"More like home," said Tom. Sam was in tears and Molly picked him up and put him on her lap as she had done not so many years ago with Benedick. The boys were sent to a co-educational school called Walton. According to the brochure and the headmaster's oratory at his meeting with the Professor and Molly, Walton extended every licence.

"The lady and I are not married," the Professor had said to the headmaster at the interview.

"What do you mean?"

"What I say. Also, the boys are mine by another lady. An agreeable woman who used to breed New Forest ponies and explored Nuristan and played chess."

"What are you trying to say?"

"That I don't want any joking about the boys' parentage."

"Oh, you needn't worry about that here. We're very liberal."

"Liberal meaning what?" said Molly. "I mean, is there a nice matron they could go to in case of need?"

"Our staff are all liberal."

" 'Language', wrote Flaubert," said the Professor, " 'is the cracked drum on which we beat out tunes for bears to dance to, when all the time we are longing to move the stars to pity'."

Sam and Tom both had long hair. In their first term, Tom was seen by a peeking master to be in bed with a long-haired older student. The master threw back the bed clothes. The two were making love. The master stalked out and went to the school chaplain the next morning.

"I found Corbett Major making love to a boy whom I think I detected to be Quinto Minimus."

The chaplain had recently sent out a questionnaire about masturbation and sodomy to the school's population, exhorting the boys not to feel ashamed of either practice, not to believe myths about hair growing on the palms as a result of masturbation, and at all times to remember that there was no such thing as an abnormality at Walton.

Things were taken over by the chaplain, who went to the headmaster. "You know more about sex," said the headmaster. The chaplain spoke to Tom.

"You're not to hold anything back. What you were doing was perfectly natural. Boys at your age constantly fall in love. It does no harm in later years."

"She's very nice."

"She?"

"I'm not going to let on what her name was."

"She? The master specifically said it must have been one of the older boys because of his long hair."

"It was a she, I said."

"Excessive sex can make your face come out in boils," shouted the chaplain. "The wind will change and you'll be left with a scowl on your face for life."

Peregrine had gone from Turkey to Positano. The time was out of season and his rented villa was high up on a windy cliff. The path to it wound around the hill that edged the northern side of the little town. The citizens went about their local

45

winter business, fishing as the winds rocked their boats, waiting for the summer to start. Peregrine wrote from five o'clock in the morning to escape the anxieties of his maid Maria, for whom he was paying too much, perhaps for the sake of her company. She would arrive to make him Neapolitan pizza or a dish of fish. His hold on Italian improved because he thought he could make up the language by mixing French and Latin. Maria felt strongly that life should consist in laughing, love, friends, babies and food, and she hated the sight of the typewriter or any sign of Peregrine's having been labouring, though labour was what she did. He became a furtive worker, huddled under a blanket beside the dying log fire at night, and sleeping like a gentleman after lunch. This made Maria very happy, but she would have been happier if he had had a wife and baby there with him. One day she arrived earlier than usual, before Peregrine had time to put the cover over the typewriter she so hated. He decided to tell her what he was doing. A play in poetry. *"Dramma in Pietà,"* he said, improvising Italian wildly, and she looked moved that an Englishman who was not a Catholic should attempt such a theme. He managed to convey that the story was set in the last days of the Kaiser's Germany before the First World War, and then even managed to get across the linguistic handicaps to explain that the hero was a homosexual. The play was a tragedy with something funny about it, he said. And the man had many friends, he said, soothing one of her ideas of the necessities of life. Feeling compelled to go further when she seemed so interested, he said that the man was subject to blackmail because he was a – he thought of the French *espion* and made up an Italian-sounding word – a *spinaggio*. Maria left more quickly than the wind, after going into the kitchen to laugh with a deal of thigh-slapping and gurgling, to tell the townspeople that the Englishman who slept all day was writing a tragedy about spinach.

46

From then on their friendship was sealed. Peregrine felt able to take the lid off his typewriter and to say that he was not married, accounting for the lack of a wife with him, let alone an Italianate clutch of toddlers. Maria told him many tales of Positano. At the top of the mountain, you see, there are bears who eat climbers. One must never ascend the mountain without a local citizen, you see, someone who knows the bears' haunts. And sleep during the night should be unbroken: to achieve this, fry a cut-up Italian loaf in oil and a whole garlic – not a clove of garlic, a whole garlic – and eat the loaf just before going to bed. Peregrine tried to suggest that this was a perfectly acceptable way for good Catholics to keep down the birth rate, but the idea did not get across.

Peregrine to Benedick
Dear Benedick,
Oh to have the Lord's capacity of language and themes, and to reduce the bickering world to order with each stroke of the keys. How are you?
Love,
Peregrine

Benedick to Peregrine
Dear old thing,
Papa seems rather poorly. I'm worried about him as well as about you. The weather is beautiful and balmy. The houses are falling down all around us. Will you put numbers on your letters so that I can tell if I'm missing any? I feel a long way away but I've been earning some money teaching the piano. The harpsichord is in a mess because an English

actor turned up at Christmas and wouldn't go until five in the morning while everyone was asleep around him, draped on the furniture and snoring, looking like more dust sheets. And the actor spilt a candle, one that he'd put on the harpsichord, straight down into the plectrums so that the top octave of the instrument is dumb because it's locked with wax. I asked a woman at the British Council what to do and she said, "Use a moderately hot iron with blotting paper." How the hell do you iron the innards of a harpsichord? I think I'll have a blow-out and get another instrument. I don't know the Turkish for harpsichord.

Love,
Benedick

Peregrine to Benedick
Dear Benedick,

Just because I'm the elder, how am *I* supposed to iron the harpsichord? I've arranged to send you one from Rome at *tremendous expense* and with *a great deal of trouble* and you should be giving *concerts* not *lessons*.

Love,
Methuselah

Benedick to Peregrine
Dear Methuselah,

I'm afraid I had to go for a walk to collect myself when I got your letter. What a present. How are you off for money? I've made quite a lot from a concert I gave for the British Council – I persuaded the dragon there not to let her boss put on Gilbert & Sullivan just for once – and here's your share of the loot. 33⅓ percent, like an art gallery, not 10 percent, like estate agents. The cheque's on the English bank and I'll never speak to you again if you don't cash it.

Love,
Benedick

Peregrine to Benedick
Dear Benedick,

I'm in despair about work. I seem to do it better when we're together. I can't sleep, which I always can when you're around. This bloody villa is all tiles, and windows which give me an unrivalled view of the windswept ocean and shivering fishermen not catching any lobsters. The worst time is half past four in the morning. The odd thing is that I like being alone usually. I even miss the noise of traffic in this place. You know it's all built up a hillside and the only streets are steps? I've made some friends and I take Maria out for a drink after she's finished, making work impossible. You should do another concert. Why don't you get in touch with the Cultural Attaché or the Ambassador or something at our Embassy in Ankara? The Istanbul virago doesn't sound too hot. I miss you.

Love,
The Old One

Benedick to Peregrine
Dear Old One,

Your magnificent present has arrived. It's the best harpsichord I've ever played on. How did you know what to get when you've always said you had a tin ear? There are

49

some ideal presents one can give different people, once in a lifetime, and you've done it. Positano sounds glum. Why don't you go back to England?

Love,
Benedick

Peregrine to Benedick
Dear Benedick,
Tin ear indeed!

Yours truly,
Peregrine

Benedick to Peregrine
Dear Peregrine,
Of course you haven't got a tin ear about *words*, I meant *music*. You always said you couldn't tell the National Anthem from *Pomp and Circumstance*. I'm feeling very buoyed up by the harpsichord but worried about you.

Yours faithfully,
Benedick

Peregrine to Benedick
Dear Benedick,
Glad about the harpsichord. I'm feeling rather down at the moment. Even the climb around the cliff is making me bored when I do it every time after dinner with Maria and a torch. I must say she's a blessing. She bought a film fan magazine the other day and decided she was too fat and went on a diet of *lasagne verde* because she thought the spinach

in it made it slimming. Spinach seems to come up too often in my life at the moment. Not much else does. I think I should have read forestry at Oxford.

> Yours in despair,
> Peregrine

Benedick to Peregrine
Dear Peregrine,
Does one *read* forestry? I thought one did it with an axe.

> Love,
> Benedick

Peregrine to Benedick
Dear Benedick,
All right, I should have been a house painter. And don't tell me Hitler was a house painter because I know. I'm moving from a period of the sublime to a period of the Gor-blimey.

> Ever,
> Peregrine

P.S. I suppose there's nothing like a little dissatisfaction for sorting things out.

Benedick to Peregrine
Dear Peregrine,
Nothing like a little grief for fouling things up.

> Courage,
> B.

8

The mails in Italy came erratically. Peregrine found himself in the middle of a strike that affected not only the post but also the telephone and telegrams. The break in communication suited something about his present taste for solitude. He began to live in a chill delirium of work. At a distance from home he started to see England as if he were looking at it through the wrong end of a telescope.

He loved his land with all his heart.

He had no idea of what was going on in England, where people in established places were busy talking about him with easy resentment.

"It's rather foolish of him to attack the money spent on clipping poodles," said the political editor of a smart-aleck magazine. "My dear and beloved wife spends all her pocket money on our poodle. We have him clipped in Sloane Street and send him around in the car to the odd person."

"It's also rather foolish to attack the Royal Family," said a Duke who was a member of the Conservative Shadow Cabinet. "Don't you think it's rather a *boring* subject? I do hate bores, don't you? One does think people have a duty to be interesting."

"Personally," said a Labour Member of Parliament currying

favour with Tories, "speaking for myself, apart from my constituency, I can see a lot of fault that could be found with the Royal Family, especially if one were a bit of a pinko, which God knows one wants to encourage in a free society, but I think Mr Corbett has gone too far over his battle about the allowances to the sovereign's relations. After all they do pay tax. If I were HM I'd be a wee bittock cross. Not that she ever gets cross. She's a dedicated woman. Very shy."

On taped TV, the same MP: "Mr Corbett has gone overboard a bit."

Interviewer: "Did you say you were bored?"

MP: "I think I said *he'd* gone *overboard*. You could check the tape. Gone overboard a bit. Her Majesty is her own most dutiful subject. Mr Corbett – living outside England, which puts him in no position to criticise our affairs, I'm sure you'll agree – Mr Corbett has been pushing it. Apart from the question of loyalty to HM, there's also a good deal to be cleared up about his situation with his family, as I understand it from a call from a newspaper peer."

Lord X, talking to the MP: "It was splendid to see you last weekend. Lovely house, isn't it? Lovely lady of the house. Capability Brown's work on the gardens is unrivalled, in my view. Give me a ring about what you think of this Corbett. I've sent a couple of men here down to the school to ferret out something about the twins, poor mites."

The matron at the twins' school was offered a hundred pounds for providing information about the twins. She refused the hundred pounds but talked, without accuracy.

When the strike was over Peregrine got an envelope of newspaper clippings attacking him because he was not with his half-brothers. Typically, the stories confused him with his father and also with Benedick. They described the boys as his illegitimate sons, wrote bleeding-heart features about Joanna as though she had been his wife rather than Benedick's, said how much she had suffered from his absorption with his work, described the rented little villa in Positano as though it were a palace. The clippings were sent anonymously. By the next post the local postman climbed the steps to the villa with a parcel that seemed to be a book. It was postmarked as being from Esher. The postman said, "I shouldn't open it, signor. We investigated it at the post office and find that it is a box of excrement." The words were hard for Peregrine to follow but he grasped the gist, and the postman spoke a little English. "I have to get a signature," said the postman, "because it came by an important type of postal service. We did not want the signor to see this bad piece of mail, which it disgraces the name of Positano to have passing through our system, so we did up the parcel again most carefully with sealing wax. You see it here and here, and again here. The head postmaster of Positano put on the seals the imprint of his official ring, which is gold, very delicate. You are to throw away the parcel for the honour of Positano and because we love and enjoy the signor, but I must have a signature."

In days to come Peregrine found himself signing for scurrilous anonymous letters, mostly from mothers, and an anonymously sent clipping about the licentious life led by the boys at Walton. He began to throw the letters away unopened. One day, when he was working on the terrace after Maria had gone home, a photographer fell out of a tree outside the villa. Another photographer was in another tree and a man who turned out to be a stringer for a London tabloid pealed on the bell and then, seeing Peregrine, clambered up the path to the terrace.

"What do you want?" said Peregrine.

"How much rent do you pay? Where are your maids?"

Peregrine said nothing and tapped his pen.

"It's quite a luxury villa, isn't it? May I have your information about how long you intend to be here? When did you last write to your sons?"

"Half-brothers."

"And their mother? You're divorced, Professor Corbett, aren't you?"

"I'm not married. I'm not Professor Corbett."

The reporter laughed heartily and wrote on his shorthand pad.

"It would be much better to be co-operative about my questions about the rent. How many hours a day do you actually do any work?"

"Go away. Your photographers are falling out of the trees like rotten pears."

"I understand you don't approve of the money accorded by Act of Parliament to the Royal Family. I understand that you don't love dogs. These are matters close to the heart of the public."

"Those are my opinions, in poems you got hold of heaven knows how."

"My information is that you are receiving a great deal of mail. Have you been in touch with the Walton headmaster? Are you a member of the Labour Party?"

Silence.

"Please co-operate with me, Professor Corbett."

"I can only tell you that every scrap of information you have is wrong. And I am *not* Professor Corbett."

"You deny the parentage of your own children."

"They're not my children."

"Aha!" The reporter wrote in his notebook again. "Illegitimate. You deny that you are Professor Corbett and you confirm that the twins at Walton, who are of course taking drugs – ''

'' – Of course, as you understand things.''

'' – You confirm that you have not been in touch with them. Our bank of obituary material, what we call the morgue, shows that Professor Corbett has custody of these little boys. We ran a story yesterday showing that the boys and girls at Walton have showers together. Would you say that that was a proper upbringing?''

Peregrine remained quiet. The reporter wrote in his notebook.

''And this question of your rent and your servants.''

''What a filthy job you do.''

''Just answer my questions. I've got three children to support in Rome.''

''Get out.'' Peregrine rose from his work, which the reporter had been trying to read.

''I've got a mortgage to pay off,'' the reporter whined. ''Meanwhile you live in the lap of luxury, writing about England. When did you last make a tax declaration?''

Peregrine roared at the photographers and the reporter. ''Leave me alone, you pink-eyed dingy scavengers.''

''I won't take any more of your time. The butler will be able to help me.''

''You must be out of your mind.''

''The paper has a very full file on your way of life.''

''You know nothing, and you don't even know that you know nothing. You speak disparagingly of exile and live in Rome yourself without doing anything worthy by the day's end. What are you going to think of your life when you're three score years and ten?''

''I've got a mortgage to pay off, I said. The question of your rent.''

"We are not here to gossip, or to report. We are here to learn the language of England. The best place for me to learn it is here."

"Is that something from your book?"

"It occurred to me, thinking of your life. You can quote it, if you like. You'll presumably get it wrong."

Two months later Peregrine found that Maria had been offered the Italian equivalent of a hundred pounds for information about the rent of the villa, the number of maids, any international calls, any sign of a quarrel that she could supply by telephoning Fleet Street collect. Maria herself told Peregrine about the bribe. The postmaster and the keepers of the local cafés had been offered the same things. Peregrine had become Positano's devoted ally, the summer was approaching, the sun rose earlier and set later so that the fishermen didn't have to work in the dark, and the village closed their ranks solidly against the strange questions of the signor's visitors. They would have liked the money but they disliked the men.

Peregrine himself was nearly penniless and his modest villa, very cheap in winter, was going to be too expensive with the summer drawing on. He earned a little by writing for English magazines and newspapers. He found a cheap way of getting back to Turkey to see Benedick, carefully cleaning and ironing his much worn clothes. Benedick always revived him, and Peregrine chose never to show that he, the elder brother, was

57

in any plight. Again they walked the streets of Istanbul together, laughing or engrossed in talk: Benedick the shorter and more strongly built, Peregrine thin with limbs that fell into loose Petrouchka positions. In the guise they presented to the world they were as different as in their gait. Peregrine was decisive. Benedick followed his lead as he had when he was a child. They made a vivacious prospect as they walked through Istanbul together on their way to give lessons, laughing with their faces lifted to the sun, which glinted on Benedick's spectacles and made him rub his eyes. Sometimes Benedick wrote in a journal about Peregrine's influence, recognising his joyful dependence to be a problem, making an uncharacteristic attempt to analyse it in a way that was both sad and tonic.

April 23rd, St George's Day, morning
 The air is like a diamond. I miss England, but not so much as Peregrine must, who brings England with him in everything he does. I wonder whether I am a burden to him? Perhaps he hides his greater griefs from me. It would be like him to. There is no doubt in my mind that he is a genius, but something is holding him back. He seems restless and I catch the germ from him. It is hard to have a cleverer older brother. He has developed a stammer since the barrage of abuse from the English newspapers. He has such a hold on me that I sometimes catch myself stammering too. When he is thinking about work it seems to me that he finds me commonplace, which I am when he is absorbed in his own thoughts. I wish he would get married to someone who matched his zest, though I am afraid I should be jealous of her. For my own part, I am much better now without Joanna. I love this sleepy wooden house and I am learning Turkish quite well, though not as well as Peregrine would

do if he put his mind to it. I really think he could do anything.

Last night Peregrine and I went out and played billiards with an elderly Englishman and his wife. Peregrine played much better than I did. My spectacles are a handicap. I think my eyes have changed and these glasses no longer suit me. Of course I am getting older, but I tend to forget it because Peregrine is always going to be older than me. Which is an obvious remark, but I really do believe it explains why I always feel younger than I am. Tonight we are going to celebrate Shakespeare's birthday by going to a Russian restaurant and eating caviare and blinis. (Not that the Russian part has anything to do with Shakespeare, but Russians have a gift for festivity and though neither of us has much money for such a dinner we don't feel down on our luck.) There is a Russian restaurant on the Bosphorus that makes us think of Sergei Sergeivitch. I notice that I talk about "we" too much. I don't follow Peregrine in everything: not in drinking (he holds his drink better than I do; I have to be boringly cautious not to make a fool of myself) and not in politics. I think I am much more to the Left than Peregrine, which is odd considering what an original man he is. I was always under the impression – I suppose this is what they call a received idea – that original and prophetic people were naturally iconoclasts. Yet there is something quite irresistible about Peregrine in spite of the Toryism that divides us. Perhaps I am a Socialist just because Peregrine isn't. I think I am probably a dullard, always reacting to or against other people instead of being the author of myself. Peregrine is the one person in the world who makes me feel I could do something poetic with

59

my life. I should like to try to compose something genuinely good; just one thing might be enough to justify a man. On the other hand, I remember the old Englishman we saw at billiards last night once put his hand on my shoulder when I had been playing him one of my pieces and said, "Output, my dear boy, output." Of course, this would be a fine thing to do on Shakespeare's birthday: to celebrate by starting a fugue I have had in mind ever since Peregrine's arrival. Perhaps it would not come off, but then I could go on to something other. This is what Shakespeare did. If he ever felt that something had gone wrong with the tangent of a play, which even he must sometimes have done, he would never revise but simply go on to the next play. I must be a buffoon to write of myself in the same breath as Shakespeare, but Peregrine's odd presence – abrasive but gay – somehow gives me the courage to have a little more persistence. I am afraid I am not a man of very much stamina. I expect that is why Joanna left me. Never mind, caviare and blinis tonight. A last word to myself: *cultivate indignation*. Peregrine seems to find it quite easy to shake his fist at the world whereas I lapse into silence except when I am with him. What cheek, for me to be writing such things under the same roof as the man I truly believe to be one of the most gifted people I have ever known.

They drank a toast in vodka to Shakespeare that night at the Russian restaurant. All trace of indecision left Be_.edick until the moment came when the bill was to be paid. Peregrine insisted on producing the money for all of it.

"I'm the elder," said Peregrine.

"We should split it."

"No. Pretend you're a gossip reporter and that I can afford to have a butler."

Dry-eyed but feeling ready to weep, Benedick said, "There I go again."

"Doing what?"

"Doing what you say."

"All right, we'll split it. I'm sorry."

They walked home together, laughing and joking. It was a long way. There was time enough for Benedick to say that he had been trying to compose a fugue and had come quite a distance with it. There was also time for the exchange about the bill to burn itself into Peregrine's mind.

9

Peregrine left Istanbul for Paris, because he was aware that he was exerting too much influence on Benedick. For Benedick's part, he refrained from trying to prevent Peregrine's going. He thought he was in the way.

Peregrine lived in a cheap, agreeable *pension* overlooking a cemetery. The view suited his mood. He slept all day, wrote every day from four o'clock in the afternoon, finished at ten in the evening and then stayed up until six in the morning in cafés, ostensibly drinking cups of coffee and glasses of Pernod, actually watching and listening. The loneliness of his life bothered him not at all and the times of his working life befitted him. The daytime seemed to him overlit. He wrote daily in the growing dusk in bright and feverish colours, as if he looked at the world without eyelids, even when the sun had sunk. There was no hysteria in his work. The hysterical punished him. He found it unmoving. He wrote with a surprisingly mild and distant gaze; unlike most of his contemporaries he was not the prisoner of his period. He detested the intensity of moral fervour that so often attracted attention to the artists of the seventies in England and America. The life of an onlooker blessed his work. The world of living in a hotel suited him. He liked the woeful monotony of it, the ranks of closed doors with shoes left outside to be cleaned, the possible intimacies going on behind those closed doors between people he would never know but always observe, as he did in the cafés where he sipped his Pernods through the night. He was not at all a typical English Tory writer of his time and it was best for him to express his love for England at a remove. There was an acidity and rowdiness about right-wing authors of his period that was absent from the eighteenth-century and nineteenth-century Tories who so greatly interested him. There was no longer a Doctor Johnson, a Wellington, a Disraeli, creatively. Among them he included Wellington because he thought of him as a poet of the time, who had caught the ear of Peregrine's loved land. As before, he found it best to live away from England: his work constituted letters home. He wrote in fear of the stagnation, opportunism, other characteristics of capitalism ready for battle, which he had found among businessmen in England. They had made no backdrop for a writer.

He found a note in his journals:

January 3rd
    Merchant bankers' dinner. The women left after the fruit to go upstairs. Wisely. They talked about, apparently, metaphysics. I generally leave with the women and go to have coffee upstairs alone in the drawing room while they're in the bedroom. This time, I stayed with the men for the port. No talk about anything risqué, no politics. Good vintage of port. But the talk was about a particular size of mail-order mail that one can apparently get at a discount by writing to Maidenhead. Every man there was doing carpentry, in his spare time from saving the economy of England. Satin-covered bedheads as presents for their wives. What an ebb of life.

January 18th

I have found a wonderful Russian girl who lets me come to her *appartement*. Name: Irina. She speaks perfect Russian, perfect German, perfect French. In bed with her this morning while she was still asleep I looked carefully at her small blue and white enamel clock. Made in Paris by Cartier and left to her by her mother. Have discovered that Irina was born on the borders of Russia. I'm interested by border-born people. The search for security seems to those who are secure a symptom of abnormality, and often irritates them.

That night, at midnight, Peregrine was helping Irina to wash up his breakfast things.

"Why do you live in a hotel?" she said.

"Why not?"

"It must be so lonely."

"Not at all. I like to keep myself ready to spring. At any moment in the night, a friendship may grow up. For example, I came to know you."

"I'm frightened you'll go away."

"But we shall both be living."

"What proof of that if we don't see one another?"

"You're an air hostess. So you must know, like me, what it is to live in a time capsule. It's good of you not to mind my having bacon and eggs at your bedtime."

"I have no bedtime. I wear a fob watch under my sweaters that tells me what time it is in Russia. On my wrist I keep Paris time. Passengers are always wanting strange things because of the time changes. Drunken businessmen ask for tooth paste in the middle of the night because their wives are meeting them."

"You come from the borders of Russia. We both live on the edges. The outer marches. I don't know the word in French. In England, for instance, the remote borders of the country between England and Scotland were called the outer marches. They were patrolled along a wall built by the Emperor Hadrian. When he conquered England, or thought he had, he built Hadrian's Wall. It runs across England like the Great Wall of China. It was patrolled by Roman soldiers who must have been shivering from the cold of the border country."

"What is this border country called?"

"Northumberland." Peregrine dried a plate. "This question of people born on the borders. Shall we go to bed?"

"Don't you want to go to your cafés?"

"Later."

Later again, with his arm round her shoulders, he said in bed, "This question of people born on the borders. The Napoleonisation of France was by a Corsican. Stalin was a Georgian. De Gaulle's birth place was Lorraine. They lived near the borders of their countries, where the new is strongest. They bring new armour which does not press on old wounds. I find it interesting that so many Irishmen in the past have fought magnificently in British and American armies. Karl Marx, a border man if ever there was one, was brought up on the values of anti-clerical writers. Voltaire, Rousseau. Yet he had his children baptised. He became a model Prussian citizen. D'Israeli, with an apostrophe – we should remember his Jewish ancestry, though he was to be Venetian – became a model English citizen, like his father. Marx and D'Israeli spoke in touching ways of their fathers. You are a border girl, my heart. I like you for the fob watch and the wristwatch. I love you for belonging nowhere. We are both patrolling the outer marches. We should work hard. We are the trustees of no culture except what we imagine."

65

"You must go to your cafés. I must sleep."

"Dear heart. And you are on a plane to Indonesia tomorrow. Fly carefully. What a folly of a thing for me to have said. As though you were flying the plane."

Peregrine got up and kissed Irina on the forehead and picked up her clock.

"It was given to my mother as a wedding present," said Irina. "She came from France but she was brought up in Kiev. She used to flutter her hands when she was talking and got invigorated by an idea." Irina moved her hands in the air around her hair like moths around a candle.

"You look like a dancer," said Peregrine. "I once asked a famous Russian dancer why the Bolshoi could do such great leaps in the air, like Americans, and he said it was because the people of both countries feel they have a huge continent to cover."

Peregrine got up, talking as he had not talked since he last saw Benedick. From the bathroom, having a bath, he shouted, "About people born near the borders of their countries. The more Heine emphasised that he was a true German, the less German he seemed to the central Germans. The quest for security seems to the people who are secure a sign of oddity and aberration. It often irritates them. Where's a dry towel? These are all damp."

"I washed them and the central heating wasn't on. I'm sorry."

"Never mind. I'll stand about for a while and the water will dry on me."

"Why not stand about in here?"

"I feel heavy. Like a corpse. As long as you don't mind."

"What?"

"Corpse. You know the phrase 'dead weight' in English? But why should a corpse be heavier than the live person?

66

People say it has something to do with inertia. The body no longer managing. People are always pronouncing on such things without expert knowledge."

Peregrine came into the bedroom, waving his hands at himself like a fan, and put on his clothes.

"If memory serves – " he said.

"It doesn't. It rules."

"There is apparently a Russian verb that means either to feast one's eyes on something or to be fed up with seeing it. Am I right? My brother's wife told me."

"Come to bed to dry yourself."

"My clothes will do it. I was thinking in the bath about Russia. Whether its strength doesn't lie in its geography. I was wondering whether this was one of the reasons for its anti-Semitism, because exactly the opposite is true of the Jews. The Jews possess great history and a pitiful amount of geography."

"Herzen thought of that."

Peregrine threw one of his shoes at her. "Well, I thought of it as well. You're much too intelligent to be a waitress in the air. Why won't you pack your job in?"

"For you?"

"For yourself. I'm not responsible for you."

"You can say that again. Here's your shoe. Remember that I love you, when you're sitting over your Pernod."

"Maudlin talk. You just want to get me out of here so that you can go to sleep."

"Little enough time you've left me."

"I hate people who are hung up on the idea of depending on what they call their good eight hours. It's not *their* eight hours. Time belongs to friends."

"Get out. You're a fine one to talk, sitting alone in cafés all night, living in hotels."

Peregrine went to the front door and banged it shut, saying "That's work" as he went. He had a soft heart with a cutting edge, and he missed his brother. That night he stayed up until ten the next morning. To write a book that he felt to make a lifetime worthy, he said to himself: That would be a holy venture.

He decided to change his handwriting. He practised a rapid italic script. Benedick felt it amounted to an attempt by his brother to change his character when he got the first letter in the new form. To change character at forty-two; Benedick remembered schoolmates of his altering their writing in their teens, experimenting perhaps with alterations to suit puberty and voice-changes, but such an amendment at forty-two struck him as more significant. It was as if Peregrine were in combat with a universe that denied his existence; as if he were trying to confirm it, in a way much like the way children under ten will mark their exercise books with their name and address, their country, their continent, their planet, ending with "The Universe".

Peregrine to Benedick, February 24th
Dear Benedick,
Irina has left me. I don't know what to do. I am growing a beard so that I can cut it off again. Is the harpsichord all right in the damp?

Love,
Peregrine

Benedick to Peregrine, February 28th
Dear Peregrine,
It isn't damp here at the moment and I keep the

harpsichord up to pitch. Are you sure you didn't drive Irina away? Your handwriting is different. When did you change it? Perhaps I'll do the same. My letters must be hell to read. Are you taking care of yourself?

Your brother

Peregrine was a specialist in desertion. It was as if he tried to drive others away in order to test their love. He even tried to desert himself, by this change of handwriting. He lost touch with Irina, and returned to his hotel life of solitude and observation. Remembering the incident of the journalists in Positano, he made a private hobby of studying the middlemen: the entrepreneurs, the fawners, the second-rate, the experts in trivial talk to acquaintances. He wrote a two-line note to Benedick when he had noticed a journalist with the head-down stance of the middleman recording a café interview with a great old painter whose face was pock-marked like a wall against which men had stood to take the bullets of a firing squad. The journalist was using a tape recorder. Peregrine detested tape recorders.

Peregrine to Benedick, April 3rd
Dear Benedick,
Noticed a journalist with a tape recorder. In the old days it was only God who heard every idle word.

Yrs. affec.,
P.

10

Peregrine said he was in Paris in the hope, as he expressed it seriously and frequently to Benedick, that the fare would keep busybodies away. Along with changing his handwriting, he changed his way of dressing. He wore leather chukka boots unzipped to below the ankle, and black and white spongebag trousers that he had bought for very little in an auction in the belief that they had belonged to Henry James. Perhaps they had. One night he went to dine with a visiting English writer of spinsterish nature and much expertise in roses. His name was Henry Throckmorton. Professor Throckmorton.

"You're too thin for those trousers," said the Professor.

"They belonged to Henry James."

"You should have them taken in. I know a very good tailor."

"I don't want them tampered with."

"They make you look like an elephant that has lost weight."

"In what way?"

"You surely recall the way the skin of an elephant hangs in middle-aged wrinkles about the legs."

"That might be my boots."

"The apartment is warm enough. Fifty-five degrees in the

living room, forty-five degrees in the corridors. So why do you choose to wear what look like baby's bootees?"

"To keep my ankle bones warm. My ankle bones and knee-caps have always been cold," said Peregrine.

"Ludicrous. You went to boarding school in England, surely. That should have habituated you."

"I don't mean any insult to your heating system. The whole of Paris is cold at the moment. I hate to ask, but do you think I could possibly have a drink?"

The Professor took down a copy of *Titus Andronicus*, removed a key from among the pages and used it to unlock a glass-fronted bookcase. He took down *Timon of Athens* from the shelves there and produced a bottle of sweet sherry from behind the book.

"Why do you keep it there?"

"In the fond belief that the maid would not think of looking behind, or into, two of the lesser works of Shakespeare. In the case of *Timon of Athens*, quite unfairly. I always think of it as a still-born *Lear*."

"Does the maid booze?"

"I think I have thwarted the danger. Why do you want a drink so much?"

"To wake me up. I've only been awake since four."

"You're an early riser?"

"No, not four in the morning, four in the afternoon."

"Suppression of the normal course of the day is a social improvidence. You should be up and about in the stream of life."

"I'm as much in the stream of life as I want to be."

"When most people are awake and presumably sitting around in empty cafés?"

"Paris isn't empty during the night. There are night watchmen, taxi drivers, gendarmes, insomniacs, lovers, night nurses, artists drinking black coffee at tables in bistros. One comes into contact with a gayer, more confident world. More free. I think the knowledge one has of the majority being asleep and the absence of traffic jams has something to do with it.''

"I can't say I approve or agree. In your old days in England you had a better reputation. You're becoming an adventurer who avoids the difficult questions.''

"I may be a buccaneer and an exhibitionist but I'm not a cynic or a hypocrite. Where are you going? You haven't got a drink.''

"Too early for me. I'm just going to check that the thermostat is working. It may be too cold for the furnace to operate. It'll be all right as soon as the weather warms up.''

"But a thermostat is *against* cold weather in itself. *You* shouldn't be looking after *it*.''

The professor came back into the room and said abruptly, "Your father tells me you've become a Tory. In a note. I should have thought you too clever for that.''

"A non-voting Tory. There's no party that suits me now.''

"I don't mean that all Conservatives are stupid, only that all stupid men are conservative.''

"You're a voting Conservative, though.''

"Naturally. That's why I was surprised to hear the news about you from your father.''

"I'm a Tory of centuries ago, which is why I don't vote.''

"We must deal with these bootees.''

The Professor went away and came back with a pair of maroon velvet *couture* bedroom slippers with his initials in gold thread worked on the front and embroidered to face what Peregrine could not help thinking of as the audience. He was forced to take off his bootees. He could feel the cold climbing up his ankles like ships' rats.

"I'll dry your bootees on the furnace. I don't think they'll scorch."

"Hardly," said Peregrine.

"We're just in time to catch it before the thermostat goes off. I'm accustomed to going to bed at half past ten and the bath water and washing-up water are still quite hot enough if I time the thermostat to go off at half past eight."

Peregrine looked at his watch.

For dinner they had cold mutton and a cold salad made of rice, sweet corn, bottled mayonnaise, green peppers and beetroot.

"The salad is my own concoction," said the Professor. "Based on a Chilean recipe." He ate thoughtfully, and then went on, after a lively pause. "For some reason it has always summoned up for me Ravel's *Waking with joy in the morning*, and with your presence the name has come true because here we are at your breakfast-time."

"The green peppers are certainly warming," said Peregrine, catching sight of his feet in the maroon velvet slippers and tucking them away under his chair to avoid seeing them. For pudding they had failed *zabaglione*.

"I was taught this in Italy. Many years ago. I may have forgotten an essential element," said the Professor.

"The marsala." Peregrine was hungry and manfully finished his share.

"I whisked it and whisked it. A wire spiral whisk, not a metal egg whisk. That's the secret. I seem to remember it's supposed to be served tepid. Lukewarm. An interesting word, lukewarm. It has several different spellings. Lewke warme, lowk warm, leuke warme, luk warme, luck warm. Talking of lucky, I wonder if we have had the good fortune to get your bootees dry because it's now nine o'clock."

While he was away Peregrine washed up in nearly cold water. Unable to find any soap liquid, he got the last of the grease of the mutton off the plates with the tail of his shirt.

"My dear boy, how good of you. The tea towels are all at the laundry. And now I'm going to ask you to be the ideal guest and buzz off so that I can get to bed and track down more about this interesting word we've struck upon. I haven't got any sheets or pillowslips at the moment or else I'd ask you to stay. All the linen is at the laundry at the moment. It saves time to get the whole lot done at once. I myself like the feeling of rough blankets on my pyjamas but it doesn't suit everyone. The thermostat comes on at half past six in the morning so that I can start work. This mention of luke warm could lead to a modest paper. Who knows? Ah yes, here are your bootees. Lovely and hot so that your poor ankle-bones don't get cold. It's because of your height, my boy. The circulation doesn't reach the extremities."

That morning, after Peregrine's usual time at a café where he met an aging member of the Belgian Resistance, he had a dream about the man. He dreamt that the man, a pilot, flew daringly low over Nazi-occupied Brussels and dropped Belgian flags onto the town hall, the Abbey and his own old home. Then the pilot found himself close to Gestapo headquarters and blazed at the building with all the ammunition he had. He was shot down to be taken prisoner with terrible burn scars on his face. Peregrine woke up to find that the dream was an exact re-enactment of the story reluctantly told him by the Belgian he had met last night. But in the dream, the burnt face in the café was Benedick's.

To make a little more money than by teaching, Benedick had taken a job on an American production of *The Iliad* that was being shot on location on the Bosphorus.

Peregrine to Benedick, June 4th
Dear Homer,

How is your work on *The Iliad*? Could I see an early sight of the manuscript? I have liked your writing for many years and wonder whether you would consider doing the novelisation.

Yours faithfully,
Peregrine Productions

Benedick to Peregrine, June 24th
Dear Peregrine,

The Lord save us, letters to Turkey take a long time. The location is conducted like an American Army unit. I am under contract for six months. How long did Homer take and how much loot did he get for it? The film is going to cost fourteen million dollars. I suggested that I should write the music but I am working as a non-speaking soldier in a tunic and running the Bagel baking unit. The Americans wear boxer shorts under their tunics which annoys the very nice American costume designers. I have slightly fallen for a girl from California who is hanging around because she wants to play Cassandra but she is having an affair with the stuntman. The script writers (four) are now working day and night on the fifth version of the script and living on hard boiled eggs and Jack Daniels whisky sent from Ankara by the diplomatic pouch. There are six doctors and three dentists on the production. The carpenters are using old telegraph poles for the masts of the ships because they think the poles are in period. One of my jobs apart from the Bagel unit and the acting is to distribute orangeade to the cast twice a day, which is no mean task because the cast numbers two thousand. The extras are insisting on wasp waists for their tunics because they say that the pleated tunics make them look fat. My best friend is one of the script writers who was a Sergeant Major in World War Two. Everyone else means the Vietnam War when the Sergeant Major and I talk about the War. Yesterday the producer said we must watch the orangeade ration because the film is going over budget. Then he came back again and said he'd had a cable from his finance men in Hollywood saying they had every confidence in him and that MGM was interested and hoped we could make a man-woman-people film with an element of *Jaws* in it. Is this what Homer intended? Please write quickly because there are no copies of *The Iliad* here and anyway I need time to read it with all this priority work on Bagels and orangeade. I miss the harpsichord. We sleep in barracks and eat in a mess room that they typically finished building long before they decided to move location ten miles away, which means getting up as early as we had to at school.

Love,
Benedick

P.S. This is no life for a musician but I'm beginning to think I'm not a musician.

Peregrine to Benedick, July 1st
Dear Benedick,

A letter from you that only took a fortnight, and from the site of the blockbuster version of *The Iliad*. I have sent you a paperback copy but I don't suppose it will ever arrive. What you describe is definitely not what Homer meant. Of *course* you're a musician. Are you doing the right thing for your work?

Yours,
Peregrine

Benedick to Peregrine, July 12th
Dear Peregrine,
It feels the right thing to be doing. I miss company. I think I even miss Joanna. That was a hard note of yours to get. At our ages it doesn't really make much difference that you're three years older. I do have to come to my own decisions. At least, try to. Write again soon. I'm so fed up with the Bagel baking unit that I played truant last week and stayed away for three days writing this fugue. I wished I worked as fast as you do.

Yours,
Benedick

Peregrine to Benedick, July 25th
Dear brother,
I'm sorry that you found my last note harsh. I am getting a lot of potshots in our English press. Uncle Clive wrote a letter to *The Times* using his wife's surname and they printed it. He said I had come to power by cultivating a public opinion of myself betrayed by my living abroad and not paying English tax, which I do. Another chillsome letter – from Aunt Dorothea not declaring what the House of Commons would call her interest, surprisingly well-written,

also to *The Times* – saying that her objections to my what she called "rhetoric" were motivated not by envy but by what she called "a dangerous misjudging of the current". It feels peculiar to be having a family row in the correspondence of *The Times*. I hear that Aunt Arabella – Dame Arabella, she insists: the only woman conductor who led an orchestra in Denver, which is like saying she's the only Welsh harpist who works in Croydon – anyway, I hear that *she* has weighed in. Luckily I am stingy enough to get *The Times* seamail on proper paper instead of that airmail tissue Kleenex, which costs the earth, so I only see the row going on days after the event, when it has ceased to matter. I have written off the family, apart from Papa and you. Even Papa sent a letter to me saying he didn't like all this political nonsense. He doesn't understand that one can be a rebel without being a Red. Is the fugue finished? Will you come to Paris after the film is finished?

Love,
Peregrine

Benedick started to talk late into the night to sharpen his wits and warm his blood in readiness for Peregrine. As children, they had had the effect on one another of making each seem immortal. Without Peregrine, Benedick lost his way and felt death coming on every time he went to sleep. It was typical of the kinship between the two brothers that they should accidentally have begun to share sleeping habits. One of the most moving things about Peregrine was that, though he was apparently enveloped in the warm world of an eternal present, he privately felt the chill of mortality more keenly even than Benedick did. He was like a toddler gifted with some scraping edge of adult comprehension. With a fond girl in bed with him he felt revived, but as the dawn grew on he would think of nothing but England, his brother, his father.

II

Peregrine wrote a newspaper piece, widely reprinted and commented upon, called *This Unpopular Century*. Some editor had Benedick's number in Turkey and asked him – not mentioning Peregrine – to write a piece called *This Thriving Century*. The pieces were run as a double feature as though the brothers were at odds. Neither of them knew anything of it until they met in Paris at the Hotel *L'Aiglon*.

"Our enemies are endless and immoderate," said Peregrine.

"You wouldn't expect them to be moderate."

The brothers went for a walk in Montmartre. The place was quiet, lying still for the late beginnings of bistro life and talk.

"I haven't heard a single transistor radio," said Benedick. "Do you remember how, in Instanbul, we used to go for walks together and every little shop had a basement where the radio was on and everyone was on a different wavelength?"

"Yes."

"Those newspaper stories were trying to make us sound as if we were on different wavelengths. We're not, are we?" Benedick stopped in the street to tie up his shoelace. Peregrine made no reply.

"Why don't you write your autobiography?" said Benedick

after the due pause. He was used to his brother's silences.

"Everything I want to say goes into other work. Autobiographies are made up of the trivia one wants to keep to oneself."

"The historic ones revealed them."

"Whose?"

"Rousseau's, Gosse's, Pepys's, Mozart's letters, Kafka's diaries," said Benedick.

"Yes. I'm not talking about the sort of sexual self-analysis that slothful authors spill out now. It doesn't make very interesting reading, in these people's hands. I'm talking about the sort of minor experiences that a novelist can see as being part of a scheme of things. In an autobiography the writer would find they had a resonance but they would be likely to sound of passing moment to the reader."

"I don't agree. I'm a reader and I sat up all night reading the Oscar Wilde letters. I believe that *he* would have found them trivial, but we don't. They bring him back to us. He answered every fan letter and every begging letter. He produced a string of wise jests that were like gold links, and they're written off as if they were prisoners chained together in a labour camp. People don't trust his care."

"You like Wilde that much?"

"His wit and his courage. I suppose I even love his readiness to waste himself on answering every trivial note. That's generosity of spirit." Benedick thought for a moment and said, "But about your autobiography?"

"I think if I wrote an autobiography, a really truthful one, and placed myself at the centre of things instead of in the margin, which is what I like, I think it would be exceedingly interesting."

"I'd love to read it."

"So would I. But it won't be written," said Peregrine.

"I'm gorged with scandal and empty of work. How are you?" Peregrine said to Benedick in Paris, losing his sense of humour.

As if to confirm it, he got a forwarded anonymous letter the next day, sent on with a note, "Any reply?", by a newspaper he sometimes wrote for. "Nothing but scabrous insults, looted for idle gain," he wrote on the bottom of the letter and sent it to the editor with his initials on the bottom of it and a note saying, "Please make a collection of this sort of craven rubbish, reprint it in the letter column with all the other mud-slingers' little anonymous efforts and end it with my reply, my *signed* reply. Tell them to burn my books."

Benedick said, "You sometimes react with the fury of a saint and the oratory of a Savonarola." That night, he wrote on a piece of paper that he immediately lost, throwing it away because it had bygone telephone numbers on the other side: "Peregrine's life is moving, not in itself, but for having been undertaken, for it does seem undertaken, like a piece of work." He remembered what he had written later, and put it into a folder of letters from Peregrine that he always kept with him. He had no notion that Peregrine had an equivalent brown leather-covered box where he kept every note and letter that Benedick had ever written to him. For some reason Peregrine kept the box locked by a key that he wore day and night on a chain around his neck under his shirt. Once when he was at a doctor's for a chest X-ray the radiologist had asked him to take off the key because it would show up on the X-ray. Peregrine had slipped the chain over his head and held the key in his right hand. The radiologist told the doctor about the problem and the doctor said, "Probably the key to a girl friend's flat. He's not married yet, you know, but he behaves like a man who's in peril of desertion."

Peregrine's financial circumstances were in a bad way, even though the modest hotel overlooking the cemetery gave him a cut rate. He could just make ends meet by doing journalism, but what he had invested most of his hopes in was a play. He knew it to be innovative and good, but every theatre manager he sent it to in England posted him a rejection slip. "Or sometimes, if I'm very lucky, even a polite rejection letter," he wrote to Benedick.

He went one day to an exhibition of paintings by the great American artist Saul Steinberg. Steinberg shared Peregrine's love of stationery. There were exquisite paintings of beautifully sharpened pencils, rulers, T-squares, old documents inscribed in a made-up script that looked a little like Cyrillic until someone who understood Russian tried to read it. Peregrine turned round and recognised a famous English actress called Dame Elizabeth Howard whom he knew slightly. Surrounded by photographers, she came up to him and kissed him warmly, or as warmly as she could under a big sunhat. She wore a red chiffon dress, little red Edwardian-looking slippers, a king's ransom of gold at neck, both wrists, and on the lobes of her ears, which she had never had pierced because she said that piercing made the lobes unsightly in bed. Her car, chauffeur-driven, was waiting outside: black upholstery with white piping, and a white poodle sitting on the back seat. He was unclipped and looked like an animated powder puff.

"*Peregrine*," she said. "There are so few English friends here. I feel quite lonely. I so admire your work."

"Is that your poodle? They're nicer unclipped."

"He's just been shampooed at ghastly expense. I'm working at a wonderful experimental theatre but I had to come over for Saul's *vernissage*. What are you working on now?"

"I've just finished a play."

"We're hungry for new scripts. Famished for them. Is there a part for me in it?"

"I don't know whether you'd like the play. It's rather odd. There is indeed a part for you. It would make all the difference to my finances if you liked it."

"Bring it round tomorrow and we'll have tea together. Have you got a pen? No, writers never have pens." She produced a gold pen from her little red handbag and tore a neat page off a pad headed *"N'oubliez pas"*. Peregrine put away his ball-point pen in a hurry. "Come at four sharp and we'll have a natter. I'm such an admirer. The address is on the card. It's in the sixteenth."

"Arrondissement."

"Darling Peregrine, you speak much better French than I do."

"I expect I've had less to do." The irony of that escaped the actress, who said, "Now I'm going to look at the paintings. Could someone explain to the press that I don't mean to seem rude but will they make a little room for me? I do hate people who come to *vernissages* and don't look at anything but the other people who are there. Don't forget to bring the script. That's the important thing."

"It's my only copy."

"I'm very careful with things. I promise to read it at once. I've got a free evening tomorrow."

Peregrine had spent more money than he could afford having his script duplicated, but no one in England had returned the copies he had sent, in spite of his having provided addressed envelopes and cheques for the airmail postage. Frightened of losing his only copy, he took it to the offices of a newspaper he sometimes worked for and duplicated two more copies himself, page by page, until six in the morning. He had to walk home because he had spent every *centime* he had in

84

bribing the canny night news editor for the use of the machine. He also had to walk to Dame Elizabeth's house the next day, arriving promptly at four.

"Dame Elizabeth is not at home," said the English butler.

"But she specifically asked me to come," said Peregrine, showing the butler the sheet of paper with the address on it and the time.

"She's not at home. She left a message saying would you come tomorrow at the same time. She asked me to tell you to leave two scripts of your play."

Peregrine handed them over, having been expecting this and having armed himself with two. The next day, which was a weekday when he could cash a cheque, he ironed his spongebag trousers and brushed his jacket for courage.

"Dame Elizabeth is not at home," said the same butler.

"Then may I have my scripts back?"

"Your scripts? That would be up to Madame or her secretary."

Next day Peregrine tried to telephone her but her number was not in the Paris directory. He went on foot and tried again. "May I have my scripts back?"

"Dame Elizabeth is at rehearsal. She left no message for you."

"Then her secretary."

"The secretary always goes with Madame."

Peregrine to Benedick, July 30th

Dear Benedick,

I've written a play. It's a question of getting the right actress interested. I'm on my uppers. That Elizabeth Howard turned up at a Steinberg exhibition and asked to see the script. She also asked me to tea but her butler said twice she wasn't in. I had to leave two scripts there and I can't get them back. So now I've only got one. I'd like you to read it but I daren't part with my only copy. You might have some ideas. I'll go down to the duplicating place and blow some money on getting more copies done. I've just sold a television play and can only afford to do the duplicating myself at some machine I've sneaked. That bloody woman. Did I ever tell you the story that Brecht's widow once told me was his favourite? At least he said it was his favourite but it always made him sad. A father said to a five-year-old son he adored, who was standing on top of a wall in the garden, "Jump down and I'll catch you." The little boy jumped and his father caught him. "Jump and I'll catch you," the father said again. The father didn't catch him. The little boy wasn't injured except by his father. The father started to cry and said, "That was to tell you never to trust anyone." I was a dolt about Elizabeth Howard. Do you remember the way we used to toboggan on a tin tray down the stairs? That's what I feel like at the moment. I'm slipping and there's no one there to catch me. Suddenly I feel like the younger one. Write and tell me what you're doing. I miss England. I miss English honesty. If I sent you some money, could you possibly come to Paris?

Love,
Peregrine

Cable from Benedick to Peregrine, August 10th

Just got letter about stinking actress stop can't leave Turkey now because of work stop concerts arranged Ankara stop Joanna keeps writing can't make myself answer whole thing painful anathema love Benedick

The word "anathema" got garbled in the cable-works but Peregrine made it out. The cable printed it as "asthma". He wrote as much to Benedick, hoping it would cheer him up. To save money, he found a room for himself in the house of a woman called Mrs Oakeshott who came from London. Mr Oakeshott had died. She was now the widow by her second marriage to a Frenchman called Dieudonné who had lately died of old age. She reverted to her first widowed name of Mrs Oakeshott because the name Dieudonné reminded her too much of her French husband, whose death had been an even deeper loss and life an even deeper pleasure. She missed England. She was glad to have someone English to talk to. The day after moving in, Peregrine, laden with more books, thinking in French, heard a voice saying "Bloody hell".

"What was that?" said Peregrine.

"My mynah bird. He's never picked up French, thank goodness. It would remind me too much of my husband. My mynah bird's name is Norman. A nice name, I thought. A doctor's sort of name."

"What words have you taught him?"

"Well, it has to be something he fancies. Anything that catches his ear."

"What do you feed him on?"

"He's got a very easy appetite. He has his mynah bird food, of course, and he also has the food I cook. I don't believe in letting standards down. I've made quite a lot of friends in the neighbourhood but I don't let him hear them speaking French. It's all right now, he's in the kitchen. We can relapse into French if we want to, as long as he's out of hearing."

"Do you mean to say he eats your dinner?"

Mrs Oakeshott moved into perfect classical Parisian French, which sounded odd after her working-class English. Peregrine felt uncomfortable about making her speak in a language that so powerfully reminded her of her lost husband, and after a while they went back into English, motivated by the mynah bird's return to his mistress's shoulder.

"You mean to say that Norman eats your dinner? Cassoulet, and so on?"

"Oh no. Meat and two veg. And then a sweet course. He fancies sweets. He likes apple crumble. I bath him once a week."

"Once a week? That's unusual for a bird."

"Once a week, as I say. He likes it. I hold him under the tap and soap him and rinse him and dry him off and let him hop around the scullery to get the damp out of his bones."

"Happy birthday," said the mynah bird, in a croaking but otherwise perfect reproduction of Mrs Oakeshott's voice. Mrs Oakeshott stroked him. "He eats as good as a dog," she said. "The unfortunate thing is that he can't tell a greeting or a pleasantry from an insult. I subscribe to an American magazine called *The Journal of Insults*. It's written by an editor with a lot of letters after his name. He believes that urban dwellers in America and England only have a vocabulary of twenty or so words of insult which isn't enough to satisfy us psychologically, so perhaps it isn't enough for an urban mynah bird. This editor says that the Middle East and the Far East go in for insults about ancestors. Eskimoes, on the other hand, indulge in singing duels in the snow. Like a toffee, Norman?"

"Happy birthday," said the mynah bird, before pecking at the unwrapped toffee.

"He's the best of companions," said Mrs Oakeshott.

"Sod you," said the mynah bird in blithe tones.

"Where did he learn that?" said Peregrine.

"I daresay from me. He always sits on my shoulder when I'm washing up and sometimes I make the mistake of using bad language to myself in front of him if it's been a difficult day."

Mrs Oakeshott went into the kitchen to open a bag of peanuts. "Where are you going now?" said the mynah bird. "Happy Christmas."

"He's very nosey," Mrs Oakeshott shouted from the kitchen. "He likes to know where I am. He's good company. He seldom says anything that upsets me."

"Shove it," said the mynah bird pleasantly. "Happy New Year."

Mrs Oakeshott had been listening carefully and came back into the room with an engraved silver bowl full of nuts. "Norman generally never says anything untoward. Nothing that he knows I'd take amiss. He's nicely mannered."

"*Je t'assure. Merde,*" said the mynah bird.

"Oh dear, he's speaking French. I don't know where he picks it up. I try to protect him from it but I daresay he listens to the radio when I have it on for company for him if I have to go out. People need company, you know."

"Have you got a copy of *The Journal of Insults?*"

"I lent them all to a friend who wanted to study Egyptian insults. Apparently they're generally insults about the ear or nose. It's interesting that the editor should think we haven't got a rich enough stock of insults, isn't it? I should have thought we were strong enough at slanging matches though I daresay we have something to learn from these Malaysians he writes about. Of course, when I say 'we' I'm not talking about soldiers, who put that you-know-what word in front of every other thing they say. Norman hasn't never heard it, not in my presence. I can see he's ready for his supper. Would you care to have it with us? A French couple is coming. He works on the political side of things, so we'll put Norman in the scullery because you can't have a bi-lingual talking bird, can you? Later on when he's finished his English I'll get him onto the French. He listens to the World Broadcast from the BBC and he prefers the news in English at the moment. He saw me upset once when they were playing 'Lillibulero' because of what it brought back about the War when they used to play it as a signal to Occupied Europe for the people with secret long-wave wirelesses in cellars or in a cupboard under the stairs. Norman hopped onto my shoulder. It's my feeling he's a very kind bird. He was saying we live too much in the War. Of course, he doesn't remember it, being a bird.''

12

Peregrine found himself, against his will, becoming more and more sick at heart for the England where he had chosen not to live for many years. He felt himself more at home now with Mrs Oakeshott than with anyone else apart from Benedick. She grew accustomed to the strange hours he kept and gave him what constituted high tea for her and breakfast for him. Kedgeree, kippers, ham and eggs with fried bread and tomatoes. She objected to the French sausage because it was so unlike the Gloucestershire or Lyons sausages that she was used to. She never allowed garlic in anything. She and Peregrine were having scrambled eggs together one day.

"Isn't this nice?"

"Bloody hell. Good morning," said the mynah bird on her shoulder.

"I can't seem to teach him the difference between politeness and rudeness. He's very intelligent about what they call emotion. You know how welcoming he was when he was saying that nasty word. And quite regal. My saying 'regal' makes me recall how much my late husband Monsieur Dieudonné was interested in English royal weddings. We used to go off for a spree in London and we'd get up early for a seat in the Mall, him looking nice and spruced up. He didn't like the English television news of the event. He said it was too full of Lady this and the Duke of that. I used to travel to the Abbey with him, of course, for the rehearsal, with a thermos of nice hot tea to keep him going and there were things about England I could tell him. He was musical, like me. It was one of the things that drew us together. I'm pleased to say I've went to four royal weddings. The music at Princess Anne's wedding to Captain Mark Phillips was a problem. The organist played the usual tunes for coming down the aisle and Her Royal Highness and Captain Phillips didn't like any of them. Captain Phillips said they sounded like a dirge. You know how it is, everyone walking very slowly. Looking as miserable as sin.''

"How did your husband know all this?''

"He was a professional musician and so he had what they call *entrée* to the organ loft. Captain Phillips suggested his regimental march for coming down the aisle. The organist was a bit upset because the poor old organ hadn't ever done such a thing as a regimental march. It has a very fast part in the middle. All the royal families of Europe came out as if they were dancing a polka. As dignified as possible, of course. That Princess Anne must be a handful. She's got a mind of her own. Though so has Captain Phillips. I think they suit each other. Not that they're alike to look at. About the face, she features her mother. But the music for that wedding was quite different from the Queen's. Monsieur Dieudonné always used to say that the music a royal personage chooses for a wedding tells you a lot about their personality.''

"How did you get invited to the weddings?''

"Oh, it wasn't the weddings. Just the rehearsals, on account of my husband being a member of the Conservatoire here and the Royal College of Organists at home in England.

The way he kept exact records! They'll go down in history. Long after the sovereigns involved have been forgotten. The rehearsals are always a mess, he used to say. Television cameras setting up the lighting, corners being filled with gardenias nailed to planks going up as far as the eye can see. I don't miss royalty, myself. I think the Americans did the right thing kicking out that mad old King who couldn't stop talking. Though I never liked Nixon. If you ask me, you'd have to have a country drunk as hoot owls to have elected him again. You could tell from the face, couldn't you? The face tells you a great deal about the character. Never mind, the Americans caught on in the end and acted quick as a knife to make sure it wouldn't happen again. I like the looks of President Ford. He reminds me of a doctor. President Carter smiles too much but that's a fault for the better. He's done very well with all that flying about from country to country. Eight or nine countries in seven days. I daresay it's done with every comfort but all the same it can't be easy with all the papers he has to remember to take."

"I should think he has secretaries to do all that for him."

"Oh yes, but he's the one who has to have the memory to ask for them."

"Was Monsieur Dieudonné a Catholic?"

"He changed to Anglican. He didn't like priests getting between him and God. He said they were in his way. He was a very private man. I remember him saying at a royal wedding rehearsal, when the Archbishop of Canterbury turned up looking like the dog's dinner and the Queen had a tablecloth, one of those beautiful Royal Family embroidered tablecloths, pinned to her shoulders as a rehearsal for the train that the bridesmaids would have to manage – as I say, the Archbishop was there, and I clearly recall Monsieur Dieudonné saying in the organ loft, 'If my faith is worth anything, it doesn't depend on him; and if it depends on me, it isn't worth anything.' He was a very religious man, in a funny way, because he also belonged to a society of Atheists. His atheist magazines arrived at the same time as my copy of *Our Cats*. I used to be gone about cats, but my enthusiasm went when I saw how much they worried Norman. Also they were part of my life with Monsieur Dieudonné. I don't like things to be sad. The thing is to keep moving.''

''Would you like a game of whist?''

''I've never played cards just like I've never touched whisky or indeed any spirits. Mind you, I was a handful as a child. But they say a naughty child makes a better grown-up.''

''Were you a naughty child, then?''

''My brother and I used to play a game. We'd save our pocket money to use on the telephone and ring any titled person we could find and say 'Is Mrs Green there?' We generally got the butler but sometimes the titled person. We'd do it four or five times at five minute intervals and then one of us, whose ever turn it was, would ring up and say 'I'm Mrs Green. Are there any messages for me?' We noticed it made butlers and maids cross but if it was the titled person he or she was generally very nice.''

Peregrine to Benedick, September 4th

Dear Benedick,

How are you? I wish the telephone weren't so expensive and so impossible to talk on properly. I'm very pleased about your concerts. If you were to ask me what you seem to miss most, I'd say not Joanna, but working all the time, from the way you write of her. The small luxuries one doesn't notice, but the lack of interest one does. We may both be badly off but we're both absorbed by what we're doing. I'm not particularly pleased with work at the moment but the fact that you're engrossed makes up for it. One down, but okay because the other prospers.

Love,
Peregrine

13

Old Professor Corbett came to live in Paris for a time. He left Molly and the sixteen-year-old twins in England. It was as if he knew he was in the last decade of his life and, living ahead, wished it were behind him. He had enough savings to afford a modest room near Peregrine's. His son had tried to stop him from allotting himself another hotel, but the Professor was defiant and perhaps hurt by the imputation of there being no independence left to him. Soon he was found and replanted by a contemporary friend who let him have the run of a beautiful house in Versailles. He never chose to sleep in the same room twice running. His friend could hear him on the move all night, lugging his bed from room to room, his carpet slippers flapping on the parquet floors.

His memory was a scholar's, not a practical man's. He would talk for hours to Peregrine, who came to see him twice a week: about the days when he had helped Peregrine with Latin and Greek, when the small boy had twisted his legs around the rungs of the chair behind his father's desk, where he was allowed to do homework as an incitement to be studious.

One day he said to his son, "Will you get me? . . . I'll remember in a second."

Peregrine waited for two minutes.

"It'll come back to me in a second."

Peregrine waited for two more minutes. Then his father said, "Did you get it for me?"

Peregrine hesitated and then spoke in Latin. "What, Papa?"

His father replied in Latin. "I've forgotten. Oh yes, my life."

Peregrine to Benedick, January 27th, by telegram

Papa died yesterday stop he was in coma no suffering stop I tried to send for you but the Turkish telephone is so God-awful stop he was speaking Latin on the last day stop he asked after you again and again I played him the cassette of your song-cycle stop death in Versailles right place peaceful stop gardens roses swans on small lake stop writing Peregrine

Peregrine to Benedick, January 27th

Dear brother,

I'm not sure there's much to add to the cable about Papa's death but in case it never arrived here's a copy. I hadn't realised how much he knew about music. He talked for a long time about the days in Budapest in 1919 when he was nineteen. You'll remember it was when the inflation was so high that he told us long ago that he had to take Turkish money around with him in a suitcase. As usual he had perfect recall and picked me up when I made two mistakes of memory. He wrote so many letters that we'd never find them all but I suppose we should try to publish them. I bought him a beautiful silk dressing gown because he was uncomfortable in his flannel one but he clung to his carpet slippers. He talked a lot of long-lost Brenda and the twins. I managed to get hold of them. His last words were a story he'd heard in a pub in England. A barman said to a pretty American barmaid who wanted to go back to America, "Well, if you don't like it here, it's a free country." The barmaid said, "If it were a free country I'd get a taxi home."

Don't put yourself through coming for the funeral. It will be all over by the time you get this.

Love ever,
Peregrine

Benedick to Peregrine, February 14th
Dear Peregrine,
Your cable never did arrive but I had a dream of Papa proof-reading his own letters and now I realise it was the night he died. I miss his presence in the world horribly and am sorry I wasn't there to help. Why do people talk about "merciful release" except about people feeling great pain? I always had the feeling he would be here forever. I liked his last joke. Very typical. Good that you could lay your hands on the cassette. Do you remember how I had terrible dreams when I was small and they'd parted us because I went to bed earlier and then Papa was the only person who thought of putting me in his dressing room leaving me with a night light burning? I used to press his trousers every night under the mattress but I can't have done a very good job because I didn't weigh much. Was there a valet then?

More later.
Love ever,
Benedick

Peregrine to Benedick, February 19th, from England
Dear Benedick,

A harpsichordist played your music at the funeral. Going through father's papers I found something rather surprising for such a right-wing man. "In Europe events make people radical. In the United States radical people try to change events." Piercing of him. You remember how grumpy he pretended to be about American politics. I think it's important to have that remark on record somewhere, don't you?

Are you working? I'm finding it difficult at the moment but Molly is being a help. Yes, we did have a valet.

Love ever,
Peregrine

Benedick to Peregrine, March 4th
Dear Peregrine,

I'm reduced, believe it or not, to proof-reading the telephone directory in Turkish. I keep getting haunted by thoughts of the mess I made of marriage. I can't even spell properly without you. I nearly wrote "marridge", thinking of porridge. I had to write a letter yesterday about a building that's being put up and I chanced "front elavation" (??) but feel doubtful. Oh well. I always used to be able to get you to spell for me.

Ever,
Benedick

Peregrine to Benedick, March 25th, back in Paris
Dear Benedick,

I've finished a long piece of work I was doing and it's a punishing and irremediable weight to have got to the end.

It does indeed feel like a loss. I imagine you feel the same. It's a great question, keeping the brain interested. At the moment I feel as if I'm sewing mail-bags. Proof-reading the telephone directory in Turkish! Good grief! There'll be an awful lot of wrong numbers, won't there, after your corrections? Maybe I could do the same thing in Paris. It would be a link, at least.

Love,
Your fellow-lag

Benedick to Peregrine, April 2nd
Dear mail-bag accomplice,

I've been thinking about life and about you. The dreams I've been having have been oddly happy and concise, not at all like waking life at the moment. Sometimes one finds oneself working very hard and not getting anywhere; that one's just hitting the tops of trees. And then a dream rescues you by its brevity. I don't have nightmares about Joanna any longer, only bad daymares. It's terrible that I wasn't enough for her.

Love,
Benedick

Peregrine to Benedick, April 16th
Dear Young One,

It's sad to get your letter. What could I do to help? I've got more or less out of the mail-bag period though I haven't got many francs left. Apparently there are several thousand due to come to me from a libel suit I won so perhaps I could take us both on a holiday to England.

There's no tax on libel damages. Maybe the truth is that we're not good expatriates, though I certainly see England more clearly when I'm away from it. I feel as if I've got a millstone on my chest and am waiting to be crushed. More weight, more weight.

                                    Love,
                                    The Ancient

No sooner than felt, Peregrine's homesickness for the gifts of the past was mended. A play of his was produced in Paris to poor notices. And there, coming up the Boulevard St Germain, was Joanna. She was wearing blue suede trousers, a navy blue blazer, a pale blue shirt with the collar turned up over the blazer. She was obviously looking for his number. She had a sheaf of newspapers under her arm.

In the dawn light Peregrine shouted idiotically, "I'm here!"

She looked round and started to run towards him.

"I've brought you the English reviews. The English critics who were at the theatre last night. The Frogs have got it all wrong." She handed him the papers.

"Where did you get them?"

"I went to the airport. They come in earliest there."

"Let me look at you. Does Benedick know?"

"Know what?"

"That you came to see me."

"No."

"It's good of you. Come in. Have a croissant."

"Read the papers."

Peregrine read.

"At least they're literate."

"You're never satisfied. They mean the play will be put on in England."

"I've been up all night. Have you?"

"Would you rather have a croissant, theatre supper, or bed?"

It was the inevitable thing to happen.

14

"A friend of mine tells me that she always has a joint before going to sleep," said Joanna in bed.

"Not a good idea."

"I don't mean that she rolls a joint to smoke, I mean that she eats a cut off the Sunday lunch."

"I'm ravenous."

They ate some cold ham and then began again and had spaghetti.

"This friend of mine also eats before she goes to economics class to keep her mind busy. It doesn't interest her."

"I often think of the question of boredom when I'm growing my tomatoes. There's some magic fertiliser stuff but it's no good; it all goes into the leaves and you get no tomatoes. We've got such an athletic situation now with the orange-juice generation that we're turning out a lot of athletes practically tall enough to put the basketball into the net, and a lot of skinny girls who look very nice in bikinis, but we're not getting any good tomatoes." Peregrine put on a shirt solemnly. "That's what's called ecology. The tale of the fertiliser and the tomatoes can be taken as the brain and all the goodness going into limbs."

"You talk very like Benedick."

"I used to talk for him. When we were children."

"You look like him, in some ways."

"Our father seems given to having twins. Sam and Tom are still hard to tell apart. Except by themselves and ourselves, of course."

"You talk as if you were enclosed in a house of your own wherever you go. How long have you and Benedick lived separately?"

"Years, except for interludes in Paris. I want to take him to England."

"I hate England now. Those piercing voices. 'No, darling, I insist', 'No, darling, it's my turn to pay', 'No, if you do that I'll never go out with you again', 'Well, the answer is to go Dutch, isn't it?' "

She put her hands round his face. Her own bones were small and looked as easy to fragment as a young grouse's. A fob watch on a chain round her neck swung like a monocle. She had already put on her spectacles, which were tinted against the sun in the same blue as her eyes. She looked at him carefully. "Apart from the hair and the brown of your eyes, you almost look the same. How is it that you've got different coloured eyes when you're so close to one another otherwise?"

"Thackeray, I think it was, said that all babies are born with blue eyes but that the wise children change to brown when they're old enough to know better. Thackeray had brown eyes, as one might expect."

"Do you think yours changed because you were the wiser?"

"Far from it. Chance. How alike are we?"

"Who?"

"Benedick and me."

"Very."

"Our eyes are quite different, for one thing. Our minds. Our handwriting. Our hair."

"It doesn't matter."

"What will he feel when we tell him?"

"What need is there to?"

Peregrine was silenced. By compunction, he thought. No, compunction can be love in shabby clothes. Loyalty? Or was that another word he had given himself to stand for perfidy to Benedick? He dismissed the self-analysis, something he disliked. You know yourself anyway, he thought. There's nothing you can tell yourself that the back of your mind hasn't realised before.

He took Joanna to La Coupole and they had *loup de mer*. Joanna said, "Why did you leave England? Why have you lived so long in Europe? What's the difference?"

Peregrine found it too difficult to go into. She kicked her high-heeled shoes against each side of the table as though she was trying to make it bigger. The crowd at La Coupole pressed. Their waiter apologised: a neat, dusty man with a clipped moustache and hands that seemed larger than his feet. "Some day we must make our prices . . ." he said, and his voice trailed off as though a short-wave radio station had been lost.

"But in that case you would lose the student trade," said Peregrine, in rapid French that Joanna strained to understand.

"Our trade, I agree, the most commendable one, is composed of serving students and poets and musicians like your brother. That is the trade we value. So – " The waiter spread his large hands, which were a little like a frog's legs. They seemed expanded by a lifetime of carrying trays.

"You know my brother?"

Even Joanna couldn't catch the speed of the quick conversation. Besides that, a table next door was full of a film unit talking Czech, and she preferred to eavesdrop on the chatter.

"He sent us his photograph on a poster in Turkey, knowing how often you come here," said the waiter.

Peregrine stared at the poster. His brother's face stared back at him: out of touch, oddly present.

"I think, Monsieur, he had said that you often came here. He wanted a menu," said the waiter. "We sent it to him."

"A menu?"

"I believe he wanted to know what you preferred in case you ever came to stay with him. He wrote back to thank me."

"He's never given me anything on your menu."

"He seemed grievous about the lack of *loup de mer* in Turkey. He said it was your favourite. We sent him some packed in ice but unfortunately the *douanes* . . ." The waiter seemed accustomed to breaking off his sentences mid-way, as though not to interrupt a client giving an order.

Peregrine and Joanna left. The waiter tried to give Peregrine the poster, but Peregrine refused to have it taken down.

"He means nothing to our customers and everything to you, Monsieur," said the waiter.

"He will be famous one day."

"Yes," said Joanna, who had at last detached herself from eavesdropping on the Czech film unit and their boisterous shop talk. "He is Monsieur's younger brother, you see, and not so celebrated, but he will catch up."

"The years contract, Madame," said the waiter. "I myself am seventy-three and my father is ninety-one and now that we are both old there is scarcely a difference between us."

Joanna and Peregrine walked back to his *appartement*. It seemed accepted between them that she should come back, as she did now night after night. Peregrine had never been more happy in his life. No, he thought, more unhappy, because Joanna belonged to Benedick and he had never pilfered from his brother. Joanna seemed perfectly content. She took a job without the proper Government permission as a nursemaid to a baby whose rich mother was tired out by the baby's demands to be rocked to sleep.

"It yells and yells whenever I stop," said Joanna. "I'm exhausted. Now I can't go to sleep in the daytime either. Could we get some sleeping pills?"

"For you? I'd never see you."

"I feel as if I could kill it when I can't catch a moment's rest for all that rocking."

"It would be irresponsible."

"I put a teaspoon of brandy in its bottle last night and even that didn't stop it. It just cried a little drunkenly. I had to brush its teeth in case its mother smelt the brandy. It's only got two teeth so it was largely a mouthwash."

"Do you always call it 'it'?"

"Its name is Jean. It's got an American film-buff father so I thought it might be called after Jean Seberg, but of course a nanny's duties include knowing about the gender of a baby so I know it's Jean like Jean Gabin."

"Why the film associations?"

"I said. His father's a film maniac. A very genial one."

Peregrine went with her to work one day to see what she had to do. The father was indeed a genial man. He wore an obviously beloved and aging suit done up on the wrong buttons. There was something of the civic smile of an alderman about him. In his wife's beautiful and costly house – she never ceased emphasising that it was hers, this mansion as neat as the stripe in a lawyer's trousers, with pinch-pleated silk curtains in the living rooms and lacy linen on the beds – in his wife's house, he was allowed to keep two rooms to himself. One of them was his projection room and another his stock room for cans of film that he had rescued from the flea-markets of every city in Europe. His name was Mr Amersham. His wife didn't care for the name: she said it was impossible in French, so she had retained her maiden name of de Beauvillage. She wanted her unheeded baby to be called Jean de Beauvillage. Peregrine went to see the baby and whispered, "John Amersham. John Amersham" again and again into its ear.

Mr Amersham crept into the room and said, "My wife's just dressing. She always starts at the time when we should be there and says, 'We're not late yet' when I try to bustle her up." Joanna had stopped rocking the baby to listen to Mr Amersham talking and the baby started to cry as hopelessly as if it were a refugee held up by foreign police at an impossible frontier to cross.

"You'd better keep rocking. I just want to show your friend some interesting film clips," said Mr Amersham.

"I'm so sleepy and in the meantime Jean isn't sleepy at all."

"We'll come back tomorrow. I think I may have a solution," said Peregrine. "We'll stick it out tonight, thank you all the same."

Next day he went to an antique shop where he remembered having seen a large-scale Victorian model schooner that worked by clockwork on mechanical waves made to rock for half an hour each time the toy was wound. He tested the boat with his hand and thought it would be just sturdy enough to hold the baby's weight. So he bought the plaything, for a good deal more than he could afford, and took it to the Amersham house when Joanna went to work the next day, looking worn out and frail. She was overjoyed by the present when he unwrapped it, and gently laid the baby on the deck of the schooner and wound up the clockwork. The baby, fascinated to be under rigging, played with the sails and went to sleep.

"How can I be sure he won't fall out?" she said, yawning.

Peregrine pulled out of his pocket two tiny safety belts that he had adapted himself, gave the baby back to Joanna to hold, and hammered the seat belts into place. "Now he'll be as safe as houses." Mr Amersham came into the room, admired the Victorian handiwork and the care of the safety belts, and invited Joanna and Peregrine to his projection room.

"I think I'd better stay in the nursery," Joanna said. "The waves will need winding up. I can doze off in between. I'm so tired I can hardly see. What stamina babies have."

Mr Amersham picked his way carefully over the Aubusson carpets of his wife's house as though he were treading in a minefield. At one of the carpets he walked right round it. "It's just been cleaned and I wouldn't like to spoil her fun." Had receipt of a newly dry-cleaned Aubusson carpet ever before been called fun, Peregrine wondered?

Mr Amersham put his fingers to his lips excitedly, and pushed open a green beige door as if he were entering a bar during Prohibition. His film quarters had been allotted to him in the servants' wing on the basis that that was where they belonged. His rooms reeked of three cats he kept there. One leapt onto his shoulder and curled itself around his neck like a fur tippet. He stroked the others, and showed Peregrine into the projection room, which was laid out with uncomfortable-looking plastic and metal chairs in rows as if it were a real little cinema, except that there were only sixteen chairs. Peregrine wondered whether he was going to be asked to buy a ticket. Mr Amersham was indeed about to give him a pink ticket from a roll of antique-looking entrance slips. "I picked this up in a flea-market for a song. The show is free, of course, but the pretence adds to the drama. I want to show you a silent comedy in which Buster Keaton plays all the parts."

Peregrine waited while the film was laced up, heard the baby start to cry, wondered if Joanna would remember how to manage the clockwork mechanism and whether she had had any sleep, and then watched while Keaton played in turn the tail-coated people in an audience, the actors, the conductor.

Then Madame de Beauvillage came through the door, letting in a stream of light that made her jewels glow and the film fade into invisibility, and asked her husband whether he wasn't ready to go. He said, "Come and sit down, my love. This is very congenial. Have a ticket as a souvenir."

Madame de Beauvillage sighed, took her place, and watched the film without a flicker on her pampered face, which was stretched over her beautiful bones by surgery. Peregrine felt that if she smiled the stitches might fall out. Upstairs, over the roar of the projector and the mewing of one of the cats, he heard the baby start to cry again. Madame de Beauvillage heard nothing, apparently, except the mewing cat, which ill-advisedly climbed onto her lap and received a slap on the nose for his forgiveness. Mothers don't always hear their own baby's cry, Peregrine thought to himself, wondering whether he should go up to Joanna and at the same time enthralled by the skill of the film.

"The baby's crying, dear," said Mr Amersham to his wife. "Ah well, he's stopped now. What an idea, that schooner! Worthy of Keaton himself, I should say. You noticed, my heart, Buster's playing all the roles. You can hardly tell they're the same person, can you?"

15

Peregrine and Joanna lived in growing happiness together in Mrs Oakeshott's cheap room. Joanna started to teach mime acting at a stage school to supplement Peregrine's income from writing. He adapted his hours only a little to hers, which were much the same as his because she taught at night and slept in. They fostered the habit of having high tea with Mrs Oakeshott as their own breakfast. Peregrine's happiness was misted over only by guilt about Benedick.

"Have you written to Benedick yet? Does he still not know you're here?" he asked her one sharp day when they were dressing to go down to Mrs Oakeshott.

"It would worry him. I don't know how long I'll be here, anyway."

"I hate it when you're skittish."

"We'll be late for Mrs Oakeshott's kippers."

They went down the steep little stairs, under the electric chandelier where four bulbs were missing, into Mrs Oakeshott's parlour. Other people might have called it "the living room" but parlour was what it was, as she saw it. She clung to memories of English suburban life, though aspects of her were perfectly French. Tonight they had jugged hare instead of the usual high tea food.

"Your friend told me, Mr Corbett told me, that you do a very active sort of acting without words. Mime, he said it was called. It sounded more like ballet to me. That modern ballet that we used to do at school is gymnastics. Are you mixed, dear?"

"No, I'm pure white, I'm afraid," said Joanna with the mortification of the white in a country more ready than her own to receive mulattoes and blacks.

"No, I meant is your college boys and girls?"

"Yes. I'll show you something interesting. Peregrine, take off your shoes. Move ten footsteps back from the wall and put your hands against the wall with your head down level with your hips. Now drop your arms. Keep your legs straight and bend at the hips until you make a perfect right angle. No, you'll have to shuffle your feet back a little bit more. That's it. Now try to stand upright without moving your feet."

Peregrine said, "That's a cinch," and couldn't. He buckled at the knees and laughed. "How can anything so simple be so difficult?"

"Benedick couldn't do it either."

"I suppose you can after all that yoga. Show me."

"Women usually find it more difficult than men because most of their strength is weight in their upper torso and not in their legs."

Joanna did it perfectly and laughed at herself. "It's probably a matter of training. I couldn't write, for instance."

"Is that why you haven't written to Benedick?"

In the meantime, Mrs Oakeshott had been laying the table, setting a tureen of gravy on the lace table-runner, watching the contest. She had taken her shoes off, a habit she had, which Peregrine had always put down to sore feet. Very adroitly, while Joanna was doing the apparently difficult trick, the old lady did it herself, wearing rubber gloves so as not to mark her wallpaper. Both of her guests, younger by thirty years, were amazed but thought it best to control admiration for the moment.

"What exactly is jugged hare?" said Joanna.

"One thickens the gravy with the blood, if one feels up to it. Personally, Monsieur Dieudonné always preferred it thickened with a little flour so that the taste of the onions and redcurrant jelly came out."

Mrs Oakeshott served the hare. "Excuse me for serving, but I know the joints."

"This is delicious," said Joanna. "Why is it called jugged? Do you cook it in a jug?"

"All it tastes like is poor man's grouse, dear, but I can't stand waste since the War and there are these hares going for nothing. I don't understand this Yankee habit of spending all the grocery money on silver tinsel and paper napkins and tenderisers and preservatives and bread I wouldn't care to give to a pigeon. It's only a matter of cooking properly and covering with a plate what you can't eat and putting it in a marble larder if you haven't got a fridge. The money that was spent by GI wives on things that did their insides no good and things that went to waste because they left them on their plates because they didn't know the art of left-overs." She lowered her voice so that her mynah bird couldn't hear and said, *"L'art d'accommoder les restes,* you know. There won't be a scrap of waste here and not a piece of paper towelling has crossed this threshold, nor a low-calorie fizzy drink in a tin can. I don't mean to be anti-American, the GIs were very good to us in the War when at last they had the reason of Pearl Harbour to get into it. Which they told me they'd wanted to for years. I always wondered whether that was a hush-up job somewhere."

"But why jugged?" said Joanna, who was not one to abandon a point.

"Something about marinating?" said Peregrine. "In a jug for twenty-four hours?"

"Well, of course, one naturally marinates the hare in red wine and thyme and so on, not forgetting the bay leaf, but I myself always thought it had to do with prisoner's food. In a jug, you know."

Joanna said "Yes" to some more jugged hare and the delicate little croutons of fried bread. "How do you do this?"

"It's all a question of bacon fat. Some people are stupid enough to throw it away and then buy oil instead. Oh, there's a multitude of things that can be done with bacon fat. I always keep every kind of dripping I'm lucky enough to come by. We didn't have it in the War, of course, because of the absence of meat, but the bones and the trotters and so on that the Nazis left us made a lovely stew with lentils or carrots. We had a parachutist here for two years; he'd been dropped in the wrong place in a raid and we gave him the cellar. He made a short-wave radio with his bare hands."

"Wasn't that dangerous?" Joanna said.

"Electrically?" said Mrs Oakeshott.

"To yourselves, to have an enemy in your cellar in Occupied France."

"I daresay, but you didn't notice danger then, there was so much of it about."

Mrs Oakeshott seemed not to wish to go back into the War any more. Joanna saw this and said, "You did that trick against the wall better than I can and I've had all this training."

"I daresay it was being one of the Tiller Girls that did it for me. You didn't know I was with the Folies Bergère, did you? Back in the twenties. I'd been trained with a man you won't know called Sergei Sergeivitch."

"But I spent practically every weekend with him!" said Peregrine. "Not so long ago. He used almost to live with my brother and his ex-wife. That is, Joanna. My brother's ex-wife. They're divorced now."

"You know Sergei Sergeivitch! Now, there was a man. I danced for him in Geneva and he taught me everything I could take in about the music hall business. Then he went to America. Is he alive?"

"Oh yes."

"Send him my respects, please. Oh, and I've got a little postcard you could send him." Mrs Oakeshott searched in an old needle box and brought out a photograph of herself in a line of dancers wearing nothing but ostrich feathers. She wrote in Russian on the back of the card and said, "He taught me the fundamentals of that, among other things. I heard he had a set of wonderful girls in America called the Tippy-Toes. I'd have liked to have seen them. They fell down in a row like soldiers fainting at the Trooping the Colour in front of the Queen when it's hot."

"How did you come to the Folies Bergère?" said Joanna.

"That's a long story. Most English people in those days thought it was something disgusting. Erotica, they called it. Well, a talent scout had come to England on the Folies Bergère's part and scoured the place for anyone who looked full of promise. You had to learn the Can-Can, the Charleston, high kicks, not getting embarrassed, not fraternising with the customers. It was supposed to be naughty by the people who didn't know but it was really all very proper and nice. We used to live in a dormitory, four to a bedroom; a single bed and a bedside table and a cupboard for each. When four girls are together you can have a lot of fun. Working in the Folies wasn't exciting, not what people thought, but glamour isn't something you miss, is it? And about going out, you had to ask the Captain even if you were only going for a cup of coffee after nine and you had to report to her, the Captain, when you came in again." She went out of the room and brought back an apple charlotte and said, "I've been talking too much. Excuse me. If you don't like apple charlotte, I've got some of those lovely little *fraises du bois*." Again the startling difference between her accent in English and French.

"Sergei Sergeivitch told me about the difficulties he had with the Christmas and Easter shows, trying to be inter-denominational," said Peregrine.

"Ah, we didn't have any trouble of that sort, France being an undivided Catholic country and very mild in its religious views, I should say. I remember we did one religious scene with a set of the Sacré Coeur when it was very dimly lit through layers of tulle. What you saw – discerned – was a group of nuns played by us girls walking down the stage looking very holy and beautiful in our nuns' habits while layer after layer of tulle curtaining was slowly taken away. When the last veil went up you saw the habits were transparent. The funny thing was that there wasn't anything that wasn't sacred about it. When we did that scene I never remember a man in the audience whistling. You could have had the Pope there, or at least a cardinal. It wasn't done to be an aspect of news, you see, though it wasn't what you'd expect of nuns. Then there was another scene we did" – she got up, having been sitting decorously with her hands crossed in front of her as though she were at a tribunal – "another scene we did when we stood as closely packed as a deck of cards and wearing little bits of tunic like the Queen of Hearts only less clothed than the one on the playing cards, and the row of us were standing sidewise to the audience." She got up and demonstrated and then said, "And the front card would fall down, and then the next and the next and so on. A falling deck of cards, you see."

Peregrine finished his apple charlotte and asked if he could top it off with some *fraises du bois*. "That's what they're for, to be eaten," said Mrs Oakeshott. "Persuade your friend to have some too. I'm sorry, Joanna, I don't know your family name."

"I haven't changed it back. I still call myself Mrs Corbett."

Mrs Oakeshott had got a little tipsy with the wine and the dizziness of remembering old days, not to speak of the readily summoned up but unaccustomed athleticism of the last quarter of an hour. She said, "Well, that's very nice, because you could be Peregrine's Mrs Corbett, couldn't you?"

Peregrine felt as if there had been an earthquake tremor. "Did you ever see a great star at the Folies?" he said.

"Now you're talking. Let me think." Mrs Oakeshott sat down and put her hands around her chin and said, "There isn't a doubt in my mind. Josephine Baker. She would come on wearing just a string of bananas and nothing else and yet she looked noble. Whenever I saw General de Gaulle I thought of her. Not that there was a physical likeness, of course, but there was something about the bearing."

After her meal and her memories, Mrs Oakeshott went to sleep in front of the kitchen stove. Peregrine and Joanna talked quietly while they cleared up the plates and washed them. Peregrine twice went out into the hall in the hope that there would be a letter, a telegram, something from Benedick. Then he softly opened the cellar door and went down for another bottle of the wine he had bought for the household. As he came upstairs again the wind caught the door and blew it shut, not loudly. Mrs Oakeshott started awake at once and held her index finger to her mouth and said, "*Prenez garde.* Take care. You shouldn't come up."

"God Almighty," said the mynah bird. "Shit. Have some more."

Mrs Oakeshott then held her hand to her head and leaned

back in her chair and said, "I'm sorry. I can never hear the cellar door closing without thinking he's still there and taking a risk. I wonder if he's still alive. He sent me a photograph of himself last Christmas with his family and he looked as if he wasn't being careful of himself." She rummaged again in her needle box and produced a family group photograph with, in the middle, a ravaged-looking man in an armchair, wearing clothes too big for his body.

"When the Liberation came he looked as white as a pit pony from all that time in the cellar." She studied the photograph as though she had never seen it before and then held it away from her up against a lamp bulb in apparent hope that some other vision of him would be printed up by the force of the light.

"You were in just as much danger as he was, by sheltering him," said Peregrine.

"Oh, we didn't think of that. Everything was like that in those days. I can never eat a meal without thinking of rationing. I still get worried about going out without my identity papers. Call in Mrs Corbett to see what she makes of the look of him in this photograph."

Again, the start at hearing the name.

"You've been doing the washing up," said Mrs Oakeshott. "That's my job. You've got your own work to do."

16

"You simply must write to Benedick," said Peregrine to Joanna in bed.

"We're happy, aren't we?"

"You know that."

"Then why rock the boat?"

"He should just know what's happened, that's all."

"Then you write?"

"It's you it's got to come from."

"I don't see why."

"Because you're the link."

"You two are linked like twins. I don't want to get between you."

"You have already, by events. I don't know whether you're in love with me because I'm like Benedick or because I'm not like Benedick."

"Peregrine, shut up! I can't stand it when you talk so." Joanna got up and walked angrily around the little room and plucked the petals of a daisy in the window one by one. "I love A, I love him not. I love B, I love him not."

"When we were children we went for years by the names

of Brother A and Brother B. You didn't know that, did you? Our parents couldn't settle on names for us."

"What a thing to do to you."

"It didn't matter."

"I love both of you. I think I always loved you but Benedick was the one who loved me."

"Meaning that I don't?"

Joanna was silent.

"You've got to answer," said Peregrine.

"Some things are best undiscussed."

"Do you think I'd really be living with you if I didn't cherish you?"

"Maybe you're cherishing a memento of Benedick."

"You sound a very doubting Thomas."

Peregrine bought her a delicate ring made in rows of little garnets, Georgian paste diamonds, emeralds and aquamarines set on separate bands and linked at the back. It was English. Life bloomed as they chose it together. He put it on her left little finger and kissed her. The jeweller took a Polaroid photograph of them outside in the street, to their immediate dislike. He had a sly, pointed face with something vixen in it, the look of a child evacuee who had lost his parents and grown up too fast.

"I hate being photographed," said Joanna. "What's it for?"

"I like having a memory of the particular things in my shop. I like to remember where they've gone," said the jeweller. The Polaroid photograph was developed by now. Joanna and Peregrine looked happy. They would have liked to have had the photograph themselves, but the jeweller seemed attached to it. They went out and ate *moules marinières* together with Mrs Oakeshott, who brought her dog with her. They had never seen him before.

"What's he called?" said Joanna.

"Sandy. The French think it's Sunday and they call him *Dimanche*, which is a very nice name for an English cocker spaniel, don't you think? He likes Sundays. He can sleep in."

"Why haven't I ever seen him before?" said Peregrine.

"He's got used to being out in the yard. He has a nice warm kennel. Monsieur Dieudonné didn't like a dog in the house at night time. He said a hunting dog like a cocker spaniel shouldn't lead a pampered life. If you were around in the daytime you'd have seen a lot of Sandy. I let him in at seven o'clock in the morning when I have my breakfast and he's learnt not to be a disturbance. You don't catch him barking at my friends. Monsieur Dieudonné was very good at training dogs to hold their noise. We had a retriever during the War and he had to be trained that way because of giving hints of the soldier in the cellar, and I suppose we just got in the habit of bringing up a quiet dog. You're very quiet people yourselves, I've noticed. You would be, of course, Mr Corbett. Being a writer you've got enough talk going on in your head, I daresay." Sandy climbed into her lap and lay there without moving. "He's as quiet as a book."

"How old is he?" said Peregrine.

"Thirteen. That's very old for a dog. He's quite deaf and a little bit blind now but there's nothing. internal. I got bothered about his age and his usual vet said it would be best to put him down, but I didn't believe him, so I went to another vet for a second opinion. That was a woman vet. She examined him very thoroughly and said there wasn't any doubt about the deafness and the blindness, and that there was degeneration of the brain but that the brain business wasn't any reason to put him down because he didn't have any important decisions to make."

When they had all gone back to Mrs Oakeshott's house Joanna and Peregrine made their way upstairs to change for their separate evenings of daytime work. Peregrine said, "You'd better take a scarf. It's cold. Don't forget your gloves. Ring me at the café when you've finished."

Peregrine sat in his usual café drinking Pernod and fine coffee. For a time he wrote in a big black exercise book from which he later typed, because he couldn't afford a typist. He preferred to work in places that were crowded but anonymous. By hearing constant French his sense of English was sharpened. He realised Carnival was going on, because somebody had a transistor radio. The prospect of the lean herring-time to come suddenly struck him. He listened to a broadcast from a carnival in provincial France where carnival was King, supported by music in which rhythm and melody were both deliberately out of true in a concussing muddle of noise. What should he give up for Lent? Joanna? He was not at all a religious man and his mystical notion suddenly struck him as comic. Other places, other lives. He thought for a long time about Benedick, eavesdropping the while on a muttered conversation between an old man and a young one. They were obviously related. Perhaps the young one, who wore blue jeans and a motor bicycle helmet, was being told by his father that he wasn't working hard enough at university.

"Failure of the nerve for excellence," said the older man. "Remember that your possibilities as a higher mathematician will start to run out after forty. Give up trying to do two things at once. You're spreading yourself too thin."

"You may be right," said the young man.

"Of course I'm right," said the older man.

"There is no such thing as 'of course'. Think of Goedel's theorem."

"Which one?"

"Proving that there exist meaningful statements in mathematics which are neither provable nor disprovable, now or ever. Logical systems in Goedel's sense are by nature incomplete."

The two men went on talking to each other in the way that France has uniquely perfected, making abstractions a matter for conversation. Their profiles were as alike as Peregrine's and Benedick's. They both had wide eyes, Sephardic noses, unexpectedly full mouths and an expression of intelligent amusement about themselves, or perhaps about the subject they were discussing, which was ambiguity. Their conversation struck him as both convivial and tragic, the sound of souls buzzing in a glass prison of a world which they cannot escape but still try to understand, fluttering without clear hope but with many a keen pang, many a rank problem of the imagination, and much fine music. He heard Lear talking, saw Cordelia listening. So we'll live, and pray, and sing, and tell old tales, and laugh at gilded butterflies, and hear poor rogues talk of court news. He heard the fallen King speak to his daughter of taking on the mystery of things as if they were God's spies, wearing out in a gilded prison packs and sects of great ones that ebb and flow by the moon. He thought his self-allotted tasks both hopeless and well-found. Men around him were reading newspapers on long sticks, drinking little cups of espresso, talking. A bunch of cigar-coloured businessmen from some other country were roistering at the bar, trying to find a brothel. Peregrine couldn't tell them apart, yet each one of them perhaps had a beloved in some distant place to whom he would talk on his expense account, miss in the impoverished hours of the night, buy something for in this foreign city. If he could get it down, all would be well. All shall be well, and all manner of thing shall be well. He called

123

out to Mark Antony. Who is here so base that would be a bondman? If any, speak; for him have I offended.

He wrote a good deal, and thought. For years he had thought it was possible to be a mender of wrongs in his own country from afar. He had gone through every step of anarchist politics and now found himself a pacifist who did not believe in faery solutions. One in the eye for Tinkerbell, he said to himself, and ordered another Pernod and a double espresso. The young man and his father were still talking eagerly, and it was three in the morning. The businessmen had gone away in a crowd of taxis to a club in Montmartre. He remembered his first efforts at talking about Free Love and Equality and the Stratified Society to a girl friend who declined to be serious even when she was telling him later that she was going to have an abortion. Suddenly it was as if, all his life, he had been trying to make people serious instead of diverting thought with expense-account fatuities. Someone, a boy out too late, came up and asked for his autograph. He would have had been a toddler in the events of May, 1968 in France, but he stood out among his generation in having a sense of historical self-consciousness. It turned out that he was by birth American. America had sent to Europe much more than CARE parcels. This boy was the son of an American official who had been posted back to Washington. The boy had chosen to stay on in Europe on his own. His knowledge was startling and tonic.

Joanna rang up the café proprietor, who shouted for Peregrine. She came and joined them for two more hours and was herself so interested that she failed to notice the cold until she and Peregrine were walking back to Mrs Oakeshott's, when she put on her gloves and wound her muffler over her ears and mouth and neck so that it looked like a neck-brace. When they got into the house she took off her outdoor clothes and then said, "Oh, shit, darling, I've lost your ring."

"You had it on in the café. I remember the boy's noticing it."

Joanna shook her gloves, shook the arms of her coat, with no luck. She got down on her hands and knees and patted every square centimetre of the balding hall carpet.

"Shall I ring the police?"

"Yes, but ring the café."

"I'm sure I didn't lose it there."

She went out into the cold with Peregrine and slowly retraced their route from the café, looking at the empty place on her little finger over and over again as if the ring was bound to reappear. He heard her saying a row of Hail Marys.

"I had no idea you were Catholic."

"I'm not. But I was educated at a convent."

"Who are you praying to now?"

"Saint Anthony. He's the saint for finding lost things."

She was perfectly earnest. Her face, pinched from the cold, made her look like a young girl in the Depression of the thirties. She went back over their path every step of the way, with Peregrine holding a torch, and there was no sign of the ring. She insisted that she had it on when she left the café, and reported the loss to the police from a telephone booth. The dawn was coming up when Peregrine persuaded her to go back to the café.

"I *know* I had it on when I left. Anyway, the place won't be open."

"We could try."

At the café, the doors were locked and the chairs were piled on the tables. The proprietor was on the telephone. When Peregrine knocked, he came over and opened the door. Joanna was praying again.

"My friend has lost a ring."

"I've been trying to telephone you but your name isn't in the directory. I have Madame's ring. I particularly noticed it when I was serving you. It was beside your table after you left. The young man with you picked it up and gave it to me."

Joanna shook his hand many times. He refused a tip. "My hands must have got skinny with the cold. The ring must have been loose," she said.

On their way back again, Peregrine said, "We should have the ring taken in. I'll give it to the jeweller tomorrow."

"Today."

"Who were you praying to in the café?"

"Saint Jude. He's the patron saint for hopeless causes."

"The demarcation lines seem to be very strong."

"It's best to have the right saint but if you're in doubt you can always pray to the BVM herself."

Peregrine realised that she was speaking perfectly seriously. He held her gloved left hand to make sure that the ring was still on it.

"You simply must write to Benedick."

Joanna started to cry. "I'm too tired."

"Tomorrow, without fail."

But she did fail, and slept through much more of the day than Peregrine, who slipped the ring off her finger in her sleep and took it back to the jeweller to have it made smaller. The jeweller was looking at a photograph in the Paris *Herald Tribune* that he quickly put away.

Two days later Benedick was looking at the same photograph; Joanna and Peregrine laughing together in a Paris street, with a caption about a ring. Benedick lay down on his bed and was then sick, again and again. Why hadn't someone told him?

People did, of course. While he was being sick the telephone rang and a husky-voiced English divorcée said, "My dear Benedick, I'm so sorry."

For the first time in his life he hung up on someone. The telephone went again and again. The vultures crowded in.

17

Peregrine to Benedick, February 24th

Dearest brother,

Has Joanna written to you? She turned up in Paris. It's her business more than mine, but write to me soon. I want to know how you are.

Love always,
Old-Hat

Benedick to Peregrine, February 27th

Dear Peregrine,

No, no one has written to me except black-hearted acquaintances who saw the picture of you both in the paper. I think I can guess everything. Get Joanna to write to me soon. I may be going away.

Love,
Benedick

Peregrine to Benedick, March 4th

Dear brother,

The long end and the short of it is that Joanna arrived on

my doorstep when I was very low about the French notices of my play and about life in general, and she seemed eager to come in, and I asked. She's been here ever since. We are very happy but it's stolen goods. I think she's only done it because we're so alike and she regrets you but believes it's not retrievable.

I can't get her to write to you.

Last night I dreamt that we were in separate next-door offices and that I always resented the fact that mine was so long and narrow – even more than yours was – and that Joanna was fussing around and taking measurements. She discovered that the wall between yours and mine was a dividing moveable wall on a runner top and bottom and that it could be pulled in at the sides like a curtain. It meant moving my desk which was built against it and it meant going into your room to see how we could shift the furniture without your noticing. Is love really so connected with the sense of property as all that? I'd always been afraid it might be. I miss you very much and nothing in the world would be worth losing your trust. I keep having other dreams that Joanna only loves me because we're so alike and that she met you at the wrong time. I'm her other chance and I don't like it. Could you come and be with us so that we are all three together and could sort it out?

Yours,
Peregrine

This last letter was one that Benedick didn't get, because he had gone away on a scholars' cruise of Greece and Turkey as an entertainer of the scholars on gala nights. His mood was one of a certain exhilaration in having cut the ropes. He had put away his framed photograph of Peregrine and of Joanna in his bookcase, upside down, like volumes of a matching set that are often being dusted by the cleaner and never read by the owner.

On the cruise, he encountered for the first time the sort of hearty jocosity that passes for humour in the lesser parts of Harvard and Yale, Oxford and Cambridge. The passengers were mostly modes of people, English or American, who had travelled from Venice on life savings and who hoped to be able by their investment to award themselves a private degree in learning that their parents and circumstance had neglected to hoist them towards in the real life that can become so distant at sea.

The scholars, who were travelling free to their beloved places for the price of a few morning lectures, included a generally sozzled English peer called Lord Chester with a passing knowledge of Turkey, an American professor of literature called Forrest who was interested in the vein of homosexuality in the Olympic Games, a Grand Old Man of English letters called Jocelyn Birt, OM, who had written only three novels and had no appetite for anything now apart from things emitting from whomever he could meet in the Oxford quadrangle where he lived, and a Cambridge archaeologist called Kern with bright red hair that stuck up around his face like a henna job on a bad crew cut or a kitchen bristle-brush. There was also a travelling English vicar who was coming half-price in return for giving Sunday the needed pat on the head. His sense of humour was well known to every reader of the letters columns of the London *Times* and he made eager and responsible jests in the face of difficulty. His name was the Reverend A. M. Shackleton and his spine for hazard was unendingly stiff. He had been at his best during the War in a fire, or now when a practice fire-alarm went off. On the cruise he would garner the passengers like lost sheep in the case of such a fire-alarm, calm them with hymns and athletic cheer, and give practice last rites to any Catholics on board.

When the cruise came to Mount Athos, where no women are allowed, the feminist passengers arranged a furious ping-pong match called "The Mount Athos To End All". The Grand Old Man of English letters was the only man to stay on board apart from Benedick. He had been up Mount Athos to the monastery too many times to be tempted by the regulations so infuriating to feminists. He watched the noble and sage heads as they were rowed from the cruise-boat to the mountain, and said cheerfully to Benedick, "All they'll get offered for lunch after that climb is black bread and a raw onion. They'll come back saying they had an elevating time but they'll be bad-tempered and they'll be hungry. I hope someone has warned the cook. Well, I expect he knows what Mount Athos means in terms of menu. Perhaps I'll make sure, though."

"It's moussaka," said Benedick.

"In that case, nothing to be done."

An Oxford woman don came back in a dinghy herself, furiously rowing a perfectly amiable member of the male crew.

"They wouldn't let me go up. And I had my cane." She trod the silver-headed cane into the wood of the deck.

"The monastery is masculine," said the Grand Old Man of English letters faintly. "They kill every fly in case it may be a female fly."

"How absurd. Think of what women have contributed to the life of the world."

"Jeanne d'Arc, Eleanor Roosevelt," said Benedick encouragingly.

"Sappho," said the Grand Old Man of English letters.

"*And* the Brontes, *and* Jane Austen, *and* Angelica Kauffmann, *and* Kate Millett," said the Oxford woman don. "Not to speak of the splendid scholars at whose feet I have dwelt and those who have now passed through my portals as undergraduates."

"It's all perfectly just, but it seems less when you count," said Benedick.

The Oxford woman don stared him out of true. She wore her hair in plaits around her head. She slept in the ship's hospital, the obligatory padded cell for any yacht this size, because she insisted that she wanted her privacy and would keep awake any passenger sharing her berth because she was accustomed to reading and studying all night. She went down to her berth in the ship's hospital to tighten her plaits. Benedick and the Grand Old Man of English letters talked, not about letters or indignities to women. Their main interest was in finding out when the cocktail bar would be open again. The barman had gone up Mount Athos. They were both eager for a Salty Seascape: a special cocktail for the voyage devised of lemon, vodka, slivovic and angostura, shaken with ice and then poured into a cocktail glass thoroughly rubbed in sea-salt. Their practice was to ask for a double without the salt. In the cocktail lounge, they found Lord Chester sitting behind the bar sipping straight whisky with a pile of unopened books in front of him.

"I've got to give a lecture on Constantinople tomorrow and I've forgotten about it."

"Well, you'd better read it up, hadn't you?" asked the G.O.M. of English letters. "I'm very eager to hear what you have to say."

"Aren't you nice. It will be very boring. In fact I may call it off if I have a hangover."

At breakfast the next morning he was even more lugubrious. He came and sat with Benedick and the G.O.M.

over porridge and kedgeree and eggs cooked in a curious grease.

"What's this oil?" said Benedick. "Indigenous to Greece?"

"Indigenous to cruise boats where they're too stingy to fry things in new oil. This has been used twenty times. I fancy it was probably ship's oil even in the beginning," said Lord Chester. "The oil they move the thing with."

"Oh, come," said the G.O.M. "Fix your mind on your lecture."

"It isn't for a couple of hours. I've got copies of all my own books to mug it up. They're easier than other people's. I wonder what we'll have for lunch? The usual sheep's elbow, I'll be bound. What a come-down. Not the sort of thing I'd wish for the Americans on the cruise. We could show them what's what."

"What?" said Benedick.

"Game, for instance. There's still game at its best in England. Somebody was asking me about frozen game but I hadn't heard of it."

"It's all over the place," said the G.O.M.

"I don't think I've eaten a pheasant that wasn't shot by someone I know," said the peer, disappearing below with a clutch of his own books under his arm and a bottle of whisky to ready himself for the lecture at eleven.

The vicar that morning had smelt the whisky on the peer's breath and had said, "God must be having the time of His life – or perhaps I should say of His eternity – squelching sinners."

Half-way through the journey, Benedick, with knowledge only of the newspaper photograph he had seen of them, sent a cable to Joanna and Peregrine: "Love to you both stop am on the High Seas stop please write Istanbul Benedick."

He tried to divert himself with the work he was employed

to do but it seemed inefficient. He played his harpsichord pieces but the harpsichord constantly went out of tune with the moisture, which was much more than the moisture he had to give it on the Bosphorus. He spent most of each day re-tuning it, apart from talking to the G.O.M. and the vicar. He would look at himself in his cabin looking-glass and re-part his hair to make himself look more like Peregrine. Peregrine was a little taller than he was. He made a practice of standing more upright. Peregrine wore spectacles. He tried himself in dark glasses, which were the only thing available on board. They immediately made him look exactly like his brother. He persuaded the vicar to lend him his second pair of real prescription glasses, which put his sight painfully out of tune but made him more satisfied with the conversion. It was curious to be going around as the double of the man he now most envied and had always most emulated. He wished he were more like Peregrine in character, destined to go his own way as imperturbably as he, unconcerned by obloquy, bent on setting no value on any praise or blame that might come his way for the work he considered he had to do. He looked at his arms. He was the runt of the family, he considered. Compared to Peregrine's arms his own were scraggy and underfed, like the shins of thrushes. He determined to eat more and started off by having porridge always at breakfast and a bar of mountain-climber's chocolate for tea, which made him too full to eat any dinner and in turn made him hungry at the end of the evening when he was providing late entertainment for the knowledge-stuffed passengers.

The woman don with the plaits around her head planned a gala dinner for the final night of the voyage. She had had too little organising to do for most of the time, what with being balked of Mount Athos and irritated by what she called the typical Cambridgeness of the eminent red-haired archaeologist. "All science and no humanism," she declared after one of his lectures, stamping on some ancient soil with her cane. Benedick had no strong feelings about Oxfordness or Cambridgeness but he watched the intensity of the woman with some fascination, admiration, and pity. She reminded him of their first cousin once removed, the infuriating Celia.

At the gala there were crackers and paper hats and presents for all the guides. The food was not celebratory: brown Windsor soup with South African sherry, fish pudding cut in slabs, something like lamb's knee-cap cooked in the eternal grease, warm retsina, goat's cheese with black bread and a slice of ceremonial iced cake topped with artificial cream piped out of a tube. All the scholar guides made speeches, of varying length. Lord Chester's was very short, torn out of one of the ship's library books. The Cambridge archaeologist's was a passionate résumé of his work on a book in progress about homosexuality in slave societies. The G.O.M. stood and said "Thank you" and sat down. The woman don said more than a word of congratulations to everyone and added that she hoped the next tour would include a woman scholar and that Mount Athos would have been opened up to women. Then the vicar rose, beaming, and thanked the speakers at some length, rather breathlessly. It was clear than he had something up his sleeve.

"And now a little riddle for you on this gala night. It came to me in my shower." There was agitation among the travellers who hadn't been able to get near a shower, let alone a bath, for the whole of the cruise. "What is the name of the patron saint of this holiday?" He gave the answer very quickly in case anyone else thought of it. "St George *de Tours*. The French town. A pun."

Benedick played *For He's A Jolly Good Fellow* on the harpsichord. It seemed the right thing to do.

Benedick went back to the house on the Bosphorus, hoping for a letter from Joanna or Peregrine. There was nothing on the door mat but piled up copies of the *New Statesman*, bills, invitations to parties long since over, and notes of introduction for strangers long since come and gone. Of all letters, Peregrine's had been lost in the post. Benedick decided to take the initiative and sat down at the telephone to try to talk to his brother. He waited a long time before he finally gave up, controlling a frail wish to swear at the operator. He sat down at the harpsichord to tune it, which meant taking off the dust sheet and disturbing an alien cat that had somehow had the instinct that this was a good place to nestle, well-lit by daylight and warm at night. He did the tuning with the cat sitting on the harpsichord seat, pleasantly listening beside him to the interminable small variations of tonic and dominant and octave. Benedick was grateful for the cat's benevolence as he stood up and down to turn the screw on a plectrum and play an interval. Finally, far into the night, with the cat invigorated by life going on in the dark, he did some composing and made a copy of the piece to send to Peregrine, who had learnt to read music. A passing boat on the Bosphorus lit up the room and threw back at him a reflection of his face from the glass over one of the staring portraits. He looked startlingly like Peregrine, he thought. I shall be sent for soon, he thought.

18

"You've lost your health again," said Mrs Oakeshott to Peregrine, who was coughing as he bent down to pick up the post. Still no letter from Benedick, apart from a little composition with a note saying "Love to you both." Joanna had run her hands through her hair at the sight of the note, and Peregrine had caught her leaning on her fists in the kitchen as though she were kneading bread. His eyes wandered, like a mind, and he saw that she had propped Benedick's envelope over the shelf of spices. She loves him. So do I. Why not speak about him?

"Shall we ring Benedick up?"

"We'd never get through. Besides, think of the expense."

"I don't believe my letter ever reached him."

"It must have, dove, or else why would he write to us both?"

"You miss him, don't you?"

"No, I'm happier with you," she said, crying. "It was a sign of good luck when we found the ring. But it's not every day you lose a friend."

"Lose?"

"It's bound to mean that."

Again she kneaded the table, with her back to him, and said, "I'm sorry, Benedick."

"I'm Peregrine."

She turned round to him and caught her breath and laughed, throwing herself at his heart and shouting, "Of course you are. Of course you are."

She spoke in his nerves as a ghost would have to speak. But Peregrine did not believe in the occult. Joanna did, at moments. She was having too much influence on him, he thought. Benedick would not bend to her.

Peregrine went to England by himself. Eating little, he seemed to have shrunk in his clothes. He bought himself a ready-made suit in a smaller size at the shop in Shaftesbury Avenue where Benedick always went. He was much interviewed on TV and much written about. In a young art gallery, he found that there were posters of him printed over quotations from his polemic poetry. He bought one and studied it, comparing it with his own face in a mirror.

Peregrine to Benedick, May 25th
Dear Benedick,

I'm in England (*not we* – did you get my letter?) and look what I found in an art gallery. The poster is a bit grubby because I was stingy and bought a display one at a reduced price. Do write. I'm at the hotel in the Cromwell Road, address above. Nice landlady. I keep trying to get through to you on the telephone but it seems impossible. Joanna's a real old dictionary, isn't she? She does *The Times* crossword puzzle every day. It's not as hard as it used to be. She's in Paris.

Love,
Peregrine

Benedick to Peregrine, June 4th, returned to sender
Dear Peregrine,
No, I don't think I did get the letter you're talking about, but I'm looking at your poster and missing both of you. I like the poem. I wish Turkey wasn't so far from England. When are you going back to Paris?

Love,
Benedick

Peregrine to Benedick, June 16th, returned to sender
Dear Benedick,
I wrote you this letter which was "returned to sender". I'm hoping that this one at least will slip under the ropes. What are they trying to do to us? I keep looking at a photograph of the two of us when we were kids. Shall I come to Turkey?

Ever,
Peregrine

Benedick to Peregrine, June 16th, returned to sender
Dear Peregrine,
Are you angry with me for something I don't know about? I resent these distances. My fault. I don't suppose you even knew I've been on a cruise. I'm beginning to hate Turkey

139

and wonder whether I shouldn't come to Paris. Would I be in the way? Love to you both,

Benedick

In the long silence between the brothers, Joanna went on teaching at her mime school and Peregrine had his hair dyed a deeper chestnut, like Benedick's. He had moved to a cheaper place, in Southall. His landlady did the tinting. She was a professional cake-maker and well known in the district for her skill with icing other people's unpromising sponge-cakes.

"What's the secret of your white icing, Mrs Benthall?" said Peregrine as she was mixing the tint for his hair with a cake spatula.

"A few crumbs of Reckitt's Blue."

"The whitener for shirts and sheets? Isn't it poisonous?"

"Not if you show the proper caution. The laundry whitener. Nobody's died yet and everyone remarks on the whiteness of my icing. It's a secret but I don't mind telling you. It came to me when I'd been reading an advertisement in the *Radio Times,* which is a very reliable paper. Out of the blue came forth whiteness, it said. And then there's another little trick." She parted his hair in strips and applied the tint in layers. "When I'm doing one of my weddings, I never give people one of those cakes that are iced like the rock of Gibraltar. You want a mixture of crisp top and lovely soft sugary underneath. You don't want a hard icing that goes spattering all over people when you cut it, any more than you'd want a hard hair-line on this job we're doing now. I thought and thought and then it came to me. A few drops of glycerine do the trick. Just a spot. Not enough to taste. But it makes all the difference. I've been congratulated all over Greater London for my icing."

She peered at Peregrine's hair, gave it a final mix with the spatula, and said, "We'll leave it for a quarter of an hour. It's tedious, I know, so I'll leave you with the radio while I get on with a few jobs."

Peregrine listened for a few moments to the crackling radio and picked up *Desert Island Discs*. A woman was saying, "And then I'd like *Why I Love You* because I'm always busy, I'm always doing something, and I want this for my husband because there's a bit in the song about *He's always there to lend a helping hand*." For some reason the eager sentimentality of her voice and of the song moved Peregrine very much. He felt as if his own longing for a pacific release from the anguish of ignorance – about Benedick, about Joanna – were being answered by the song in the woman's own kind of hieroglyphics. "The expedition of my violent love/Outran the causer, reason," he remembered from school.

The landlady came back into the bathroom where she was doing the tinting, parted Peregrine's hair in several places, seemed satisfied, and rinsed it. She said, "Would you object to a blow hairdryer? I wouldn't like to see you catching cold, coming from foreign places."

"It's hot here, though."

"Hotter where you came from, I'll be bound."

"Why would I object to a hairdryer?"

"Some people think it isn't British. I've heard people say it reminds them of Italy. To my mind the blowdry's as British as roast beef. An American friend of mine tells me it's taken on in the United States. I daresay you've been there, being travelled."

"Yes, I have. Twice. Work."

She held the dryer away from his head for a moment, testing the temperature in case it was too hot, and then said, "Work, work, work, worry, worry, worry, and then you're dead,'' perfectly cheerfully. "What is your particular line, if I may ask? Brain-work, I can tell that, you're thinking all the time, I envy in you that ability.''

"I'd never have hit on the Reckitt's Blue idea.''

"I will say that was one of my moments. But you'd have thought of it in a flash if your mind was on icing. What is your field in particular?''

"Politics, I suppose.''

"Ah.''

"And music.'' What made him pretend to that? Confusion with Benedick. What to do?

"You'll have noticed my late husband's piano in the lounge. Would you give me a tune when your hair's dry?''

"I'm rather out of practice, but I'll play you a cassette of something I once wrote.'' No, something that Benedick had written. The landlady finished drying his hair and he went for his cassette machine. She listened augustly to the tape, hands folded in her lap and legs neatly together, like the Queen. She nodded in time to the music. "You wrote that?''

"Well, it was mostly my younger brother.'' The truth came and went as if it were mercury sliding about on a tray.

"I've been to America,'' she said unexpectedly. "We had the most wonderful luck on a premium bond when my husband was alive and we went across the Atlantic and then all the way across the States by a car we picked up for a song. Second-hand cars go for nothing in America, don't they? We took my husband's best friend and his wife. Oh, it was a game! When we got to San Francisco I swear I never was so tickled to see a place in all my life. If we made a hundred miles in a day, the men would get out in front of the cars and throw their caps in the air. Some of the roads were so bad, and made worse by cars getting stuck and grinding their wheels into the sand, that we'd get off the road and drive beside it in a field out of appreciation for the lovely countryside. If we made a hundred and *fifty* miles in a day we'd throw our slippers back at the men to keep up with the caps. We were just girls at the time and everyone was poor. I get so cross now when I hear people going on about eviction. Listen, in the thirties, how many other people in the country could say they weren't going to lose their jobs, their homes, get evicted in a general sort of way from everything they had? I ask you. In those days we had a lot of fun and we were all fools. Well, now I'm a little bit old but I'm not worn out."

"You work all the time."

"People are lucky when they work all the time, aren't they? Teachers, writers, musicians I daresay, doctors. Anyone with a profession is to be envied. Unskilled labour can get so much an hour in a boom period but they don't work all the time. If you were to ask me what I've missed most of my life, I'd say first my husband, whose death was a bad blow coming as it did just after we'd lost our first-born in the War, and second working all the time. I'm very fortunate in having all this work to do now, day in day out. In the case of a Depression, the little treats you don't notice, but the lack of interest you do. Now, tell me about your brother. I can see you're very fond of him."

"He lives in Turkey. He's a musician. He's younger than I am, as I said."

"Does he feature you?"

"Almost exactly. He's a bit thinner than I am. He doesn't have to wear spectacles and he has blue eyes. He's very quiet."

"I like that. I talk too much. Sometimes I sound like a television. This violence on television, it's nothing to have in the house. The news alone is full enough of misfortune and tragedies. I wonder what your brother would think of your hair. What colour is his?"

"Exactly the same as you've made mine."

"It's just a touch different from what it was. It doesn't alter your looks. Take off your spectacles so that I can imagine him." She squinted at the sight, holding up her hands around her eyes as if to make a framed photograph, and then nodded in satisfaction. "I can just picture him. Is he wed?"

"He used to be, but his wife left him."

"What a pity. Was she a, you know, a bitch?"

"Oh no." His mind ran on as if he were rushing to Joanna up a railway platform. "Not at all."

"She's a friend of yours? It's not every day you lose a friend. What did she look like?"

"Tall, but not as tall as my brother or me. The most beautiful black hair that falls over her face. She runs her hands through it when she's talking about something that's important to her. She has very fine legs. I once saw her in jodhpurs and they suited her. They don't suit many women. Long thighs. She has a habit of lifting her eyebrows when she's laughing at something."

"You're talking about her in the present, I notice. You see her."

"I hope so."

"One can have a close link with an in-law."

"I hope so."

"Even an ex in-law."

"I hope so."

"You've said you hope so three times. You shouldn't be in doubt, a man like you. Have you and your brother had a row?"

"I hope not."

"It's a terrible thing, not to be sure of a link. My husband and I were very closely linked even as to our ages. If he was alive now he'd be seventy-seven and I'm seventy-six and a half. He lost the use of his right leg long before he died. It's bad to lose mobility. Now television is my means of company. You wonder what these young public people you never meet are thinking. You've got to remember when you're getting old that young people don't like you, they haven't got as much time as you, that's why they avoid you. But *you* wouldn't be lonely, not with your work and your thoughts. In life sometimes you're backed into a corner. You have to decide what's decent."

"What do you mean?"

"I'm trying to decide whether it's decent to ask you a question."

"Anything you want. I can always say no."

"Shouldn't you be married?"

"No."

"Why?"

"Because the woman I'm in love with is in love with someone else I love."

"That's what I thought."

Again Peregrine's mind fled to Joanna, as if she were running to meet him after a journey.

19

In the eye-doctor's surgery, Peregrine said, "I've come to you about my spectacles."

"What seems to be wrong with them?"

"They keep falling off when I read."

"A little adjustment. First let's see if your eyes have changed. When were these prescribed?"

"Five years ago."

"Put them on and read me the bottom line of this chart."

"I can't. I feel as if I'm squinting."

"The row above."

"Will you come to a – I'm faking it – party on Saturday night. Is it party? Or binge?"

The eye-doctor laughed and said, "Now take off these glasses and read from this chart. The bottom row, first. Can we see anything?"

"A, F, 4, 5, F, 0, 9, Y."

"You've got no business coming to an opthalmologist. You've got the best eyes that have come through this door for many a moon." The cheerful doctor laughed. "But as well to be sure." Then he tested Peregrine's near eyesight, with and without glasses, giving him the same result. He went through other tests meticulously for half an hour and then leant back and said, "My practical clinical suggestion, sir, is that you put your spectacles into their case and drop them into the sea."

"What would you think of contact lenses?"

"No need. A waste of money."

"Blue lenses, to change the colour of my eyes."

"Are you an actor?"

"I'm tired of having brown eyes."

"Medicine is not a frivolous or cosmetic matter."

"It's for a serious reason. I want to look different."

"What is your line of work? There are some opthalmologists who do this sort of thing, but I won't meddle with politics."

"If you mean am I a spy, the answer is no. I'm just eager to look like someone else."

"For what reason?"

"I'm tired of myself, I said."

"I'd have to have more information. I'm sorry."

Peregrine realised that he would have to explore different landscapes. If he was suspected of seedy intentions, then he needed a seedy eye-doctor. Eventually he found one, in Southall itself. Even the man's brass plate was unpolished. His rooms smelt of anaesthetic and Peregrine wondered whether he practised dentistry or surgery illegally. His name was Doctor James Ivan Wellington, which sounded an improbable name for a man in Southall. He turned out to be Indian and kindly.

"Ah yes, I think we can fix you up okay. We'll just do a little testing. Will you kindly sit here, please?"

Again the tests of Peregrine's eyesight, just as meticulously done as by the first doctor.

"You are in no need of spectacles but you say you want contact lenses."

"Yes, please. I want to change the colour of my eyes."

The doctor was so patently honest that Peregrine regretted

having given a false name. "I want to look like someone else for private reasons."

"What reasons?"

"They're hard to explain. I'm not a criminal."

"You are beginning to get my shackles up."

"I hope neither of us is in shackles, Doctor Wellington."

"Excuse me. I am in a state of law and order and I would wish this for all my patients, too."

"A very bright blue."

"Come back on Thursday. These are not things to play around with." Doctor Wellington did some more tests, spoke seriously of world events, sighed, and said, "You have landed me with a very hot potato on my doorstep. I don't generally prescribe for cosmetic purposes, but I can grasp that this is in some way an earnest matter for you and I would not cross to the other side of the road in the case of a man in need. So we shall see what we shall see. Which is a funny thing to say in the matter of contact lenses." The gaunt man laughed at himself and offered Peregrine a peppermint. "I find they clear away the smell of anaesthetics. My colleague upstairs is a dentist and I am afraid the smell absolutely permeates the waiting room."

Back in France, Peregrine restrained himself from going to Mrs Oakeshott's and instead went to his old hotel and tried to telephone Benedick in Turkey, for the nth time. At last he got an answer; still not from Benedick, as he expected, but from someone who at least spoke French and even a little Russian. Benedick was indeed in Paris. The voice said that he had gone to see his brother.

Peregrine was at a disadvantage because one of his contact

lenses had fallen out. He could still see perfectly well, but a contact lens is a small thing to find. At the moment he looked to himself like a cat that had been born with one blue eye and one brown. He crawled over the sparse carpet of his hotel room, aware of this disfigurement that held him so literally suspended half-way between himself and his brother. It was as if he were a woman who had mistaken the time and put her hair in curlers an hour too late to see her lover. He thought of Joanna, and telephoned her intending to make it seem that he was stuck at London Airport. He made himself feel like a hunted man. But there was no answer. She and Benedick must be out, he thought. They belong to each other, he thought. Both of his eyes ached, for different reasons. He lay down to sleep and dreamt of the surface of the earth, glittering with separate elements.

Next morning the sunlight caught a tiny gleam from his lost contact lens. He put it in too fast, with carpet hairs clinging to it, and his eye streamed. He couldn't go to see Benedick and Joanna as if he had been distressed. After a time, he took stock of the situation and read a book in a café most of the night. He found himself in retreat in his own territory, hiding from the two people he loved best at the time he liked best. He inspected his hair in a looking-glass. He went to an all-night cinema. It seemed to him desolate. He became transfixed by a man with spectacles watching the film with no more interest than he. He moved up a few rows and it was, of course, Benedick. He tapped him on the shoulder. They looked at each other, mirror images of each other: Benedick become like he, with spectacles, standing taller; he become like Benedick, with blue eyes, slumping.

"This is a lousy film," said Benedick, as if he had been expecting him, which is the way of such happenings. "I was going to sleep before you tapped me on the shoulder. I'm not used to going to films in the middle of the night."

"Where's Joanna?"

"At your place in bed, I should think."

Neither of them remarked on their changes of appearance. Both had made it, so both expected it of the other.

"We'll go and wake her. We'll get some hot brioches."

They shopped together in Paris for freshly ground coffee beans and farm butter and honey and brioches. They were happy. It was as if they had never been away from each other. Nothing needed explaining.

"I've been playing your cassette," said Peregrine.

"I've been reading you in the English papers," said Benedick. "I knew you'd come."

"I wonder how Sam and Tom are."

"With each other, I hope."

Together they woke Joanna up with a breakfast tray for the three of them at Mrs Oakeshott's, who was not yet awake.

"Hell!" Joanna said, looking from Benedick to Peregrine and back again. "What sort of trick are you playing?" She caused them a sorry pang with her response. They stared from one to the other. Then she laughed and kissed them both and spilled the coffee. Her eye make-up, left on from the short night before, was running with tears. Of pleasure or chagrin: it was hard to tell. She seemed cheered by the accident with the coffee. Something for her to do. But who will ever know which brother she was angry with and which one she loved? Both, in both cases, it seemed, as is the way of things.